PRAISE FOR
SECRETS BARED & TRENTON'S TERMS

"Anne Rainey is a goddess when it comes to writing journeys of sensual discovery for her characters. Gideon is a walking, talking cloud of sexuality. One moment he is a storm of passion and the next he is gentle and seductive. The romance that explodes between Lori and Gideon will leave you breathless and craving someone to love!"
~*Romance Junkies*

"The Emperor: Secrets Bared is a book that cries out for your attention,. It has a theme that entices, characters that enthrall...I hope it is the first of many more like it from Ms Anne Rainey. A read you don't want to miss if you enjoy that touch of the erotic, the flavour of decadent writing, and a tale to make you want more. This book has it all!"
~*The Romance at Heart*

"The Emperor: Trenton's Terms is sweet and passionate and left me craving more from Kelley Nyrae. She totally bewitched this reader with her wonderful and heartfelt characters and sinfully decadent storyline."
~ *Manic Readers*

"Kelley Nyrae brings to life two enchanting characters, strong willed and well matched, Sydney and Trenton will entice and cajole you into believing in love at first sight, and in the forces that drive one soul to find another."
~*Romance at Heart*

TEASE Dark Tarot
THE EMPEROR

Secrets Bared
ANNE RAINEY

Trenton's Terms
KELLEY NYRAE

TEASE PUBLISHING
www.teasepublishingllc.com

This is a work of fiction. Names, characters, places, and incidents are products of the author's imagination or are used fictitiously and are not to be construed as real. Any resemblance to actual events, locales, organizations, or persons, living or dead, is entirely coincidental.

Tease Dark Tarot: Secrets Bared
A Tease Publishing Book/E book

Copyright© 2008 Anne Rainey
Cover Artist: Kendra Egert
Interior text design: Stacee Sierra

Tease Dark Tarot: Trenton's Terms
A Tease Publishing Book/E book

Copyright© 2007 Kelley Nyrae
Cover Artist: Kendra Egert
Interior text design: Stacee Sierra

Print ISBN: 978-1-934678-56-5

All rights reserved. No part of this book may be used or reproduced electronically or in print without written permission, except in the case of brief quotations embodied in reviews.
Tease Publishing LLC
www.teasepublishingllc.com
PO BOX 234
Swansboro, North Carolina 28584-0234

Tease and the T logo is © Tease Publishing LLC. All rights reserved.

TEASE Dark Tarot

Secrets Bared

ANNE RAINEY

TEASE PUBLISHING
www.teasepublishingllc.com

For my mom. You're my best friend and I'm glad I have you in my life. This story wouldn't have happened if you hadn't taught all your kids to think outside the box. I love you more every day.

To my readers. I firmly believe we all have a little psychic ability and someday we'll be taught how to tap into it. For now, I hope Gideon Adrian's mischievous mind is entertainment enough!

Chapter One

He could hear her every thought. She was driving him mad, and he didn't even know her name. That would change, he'd see to it. He wanted to know every tiny thing about her.

All Gideon had to do now was find her, which was a joke because he didn't have a clue what she looked like. For all he knew she was some old woman with weathered skin and a face like his first grade teacher, Ms. Frasier. Behind her back, all the kids had called her Old Lady Stoneface because she'd sported a permanent scowl. He always wondered why she'd become a schoolteacher. She should have been a drill sergeant.

As he strolled around the room, Gideon constantly scanned the crowd for the one woman whose naughty thoughts had him tied in knots. In his soul, he knew he'd recognize her the instant he spotted her. It was only a matter of time. He planned to make her every erotic fantasy come to life.

In the normal scheme of things, Gideon hated large crowds. He steered clear of anything larger than fifty people. Considering the party was in his honor, he'd been compelled to at least make an appearance, even though his heart just wasn't in it. It hadn't been for a long time. He was bored with his work, bored with his house, bored to hell and back with life. Coming to the party was supposed to be a refreshing change of pace.

Another of her thoughts flitted through his mind and Gideon groaned. If she didn't stop thinking about sex, he was going to go insane. Her mind kept conjuring up different scenarios, and he desperately wanted to be the man starring in them.

Anticipation lanced through him. It'd been so long since he'd been excited about anything, much less a woman. Gideon was tired of being alone. No one knew lonely the way he did. Hell, if he could be in a room with over two hundred people, all of them sipping wine, chatting with friends, flirting outrageously, and still feel alone, he knew there was no hope for him.

Most of his friends and associates knew he preferred solitude to parties and crowds. But he knew the woman was unlike any of these people. She was not in her element. Gideon knew because she kept thinking herself inadequate. A *fish out of water*, were her exact thoughts. She wanted nothing more than to leave and just forget the whole stupid idea. Gideon idly wondered exactly what *the whole idea* entailed. There was an urgency about her, and he had a feeling she was trying to find a gracious way to escape. But he wouldn't let her. She wasn't getting away from him. He knew her every desire, her every wish, and for some damn reason, she intrigued the hell out of him.

Gideon vowed she wouldn't leave the party without him.

He walked over to the bar and ordered a beer. When he turned around and lazily leaned against the sturdy oak, his eyes roamed cunningly around the room once more. Then he spotted her. He knew it was her, and she didn't look a damn thing like Mrs. Frasier. Christ, she was perfect. Every man's fantasy. *His* fantasy. This woman was the very definition of voluptuous temptation.

Gideon had been with women of all shapes and sizes. He'd seen the starving models naked. He'd seen the girl-next-door scream his name in ecstasy. He'd even seen the straight-as-a-pin ones beg to be fucked. But none compared. And she was still fully clothed. A minor detail he'd rectify soon.

She wore a black dress, and Gideon didn't have to read the label to know it was silk. He could see by the way the dress moved with her, as if pleased as punch to be covering such soft skin. The front was scoop-necked and hugged her figure beautifully. God, she was gorgeous. Why did she think she lacked appeal?

From his vantage point, it seemed she had every curve and valley just where they ought to be. Her breasts alone could make a man whimper. Large, round, juicy tits he wanted to lick and suck. They filled out the top half of the dress, creating a nice amount of cleavage. He'd never given any one particular body part much thought before. He liked every inch of the female form. Now he was definitely a breast man.

He pulled his gaze away from her chest; getting a hard-on in the middle of a crowded room was not part of the plan he turned around to grab his beer. He needed to cool off. Cool off and slow down, or he'd embarrass them both.

He turned back to the woman who had his libido in overdrive and allowed his eyes to travel the length of her. When he reached her legs, he had to stifle a groan of pleasure. Though she wasn't supermodel tall, she still had legs that would wrap nicely around even his huge body. Sweetly displayed in a pair of black pumps, her legs were sexy and strong and lean. Just right for what he had in mind. For what *she* had in mind. Naughty girl thoughts ran around in her head. Gideon smiled as he pushed away from the bar. He couldn't wait to make those thoughts come to life.

For a second, Gideon felt the tiniest bit guilty for reading her mind. It was an invasion of privacy, and usually he kept strict to his code of honor. But with her, rules went out the window. There were no holds barred. He had to have her. Simple as that.

His steps faltered the closer he got. She was even more beautiful up close with her oval face and honey-blonde hair. Honey that dribbled down past her shoulders, held securely in place by a metal clip. He wanted to see her hair hanging loose, spilling down her back. Then Gideon noticed she was staring right back. When she smiled, his heart sped up.

Christ, he was a goner.

***

Lori had no idea what she was doing. She was way out of her element. These people were in a different league. They were classy, sophisticated. She was plain and boring. Painfully normal. She'd only agreed to come because her art-teaching friend, Margaret, had talked her into it. Of course, Margaret had abandoned her the instant they'd arrived. Damn her. Someone had grabbed and flitted her away. How was she supposed to find the blasted woman in such a large crowd? It was wall-to-wall bodies.

She only wanted to go home. These people lived a different life. She enjoyed Margaret's company, but this yuppie world was not Lori's style. In the back of her mind, she knew the real reason she'd come tonight, and it hadn't been because of Margaret. Now she wanted to forget the stupid idea and go home where things were normal.

Unfortunately, Margaret had driven, which left Lori somewhat stranded. She was forced to talk to people she didn't know, smile when she didn't feel like smiling, and drink champagne, which she now knew tasted horrible. If she ever drank alcohol, it was to tip back a cold, light beer on a hot summer evening. She'd never tasted champagne before tonight. Apparently, she hadn't been missing a damn thing.

In her search for Margaret, she ended up telling yet another oversexed man, thanks but no thanks. When she turned to go to the bathroom as a means of escape—and call her sister, Tabby—Lori saw the most gorgeous man she'd ever seen. And the biggest. In fact, he was a little scary—over six foot six easy, with shoulders a linebacker only dreamed of and hair the color of night. The closer he got, the more she could see he had chiseled features that would rival a Greek God. He was completely underdressed in a pair of black slacks and a simple white T-shirt that showed off his muscles to perfection. His shiny black hair was entirely too long for today's standards, falling just below his shoulders. He looked like a disreputable pirate.

Oh yeah, definitely a hottie.

At the same time Lori thought the word, his brow arched up in inquiry, as if he could read her mind. As if he knew she was thinking about him. "Oh great, terrific impression," she mumbled under her breath.

Lori breathed deeply, resisted the urge to run and hide, then stood up straighter as he approached. Slouching added pounds, and she definitely didn't wish for more of those. He reached his hand out to her and spoke.

"My name is Gideon Adrian and you are?"

Have mercy. His voice should have been bottled to preserve its flawlessness. She could listen to him talk for hours. Lori wondered what he sounded like during sex. She'd bet her bottom dollar, he could make a woman climax just by whispering in her ear. Then she realized she was clinging to his hand. Damn it. She made a valiant effort to give it back to him, but he appeared to be in no hurry. Instead, she answered his question and opted to leave her hand right where it was.

"I'm Lori Fontaine. It's very nice to meet you, Mr. Adrian."

Then it hit her. Gideon Adrian was the world-renowned sculptor. The party was in his honor. She had seen his work. She couldn't actually afford it, but she'd seen it. Lori was dutifully impressed. He sculpted couples. In particular, erotic poses of men and women wrapped up in each other, embracing, making love. He was a wild sensation in the art world.

Lori looked pointedly down at their hands, then back up at him. He didn't seem to get the message because he still held her firmly. The gorgeous hunk stared into her eyes as if he could see into her very soul. Tingles ran up and down her spine.

To break the silence, Lori decided to let him know what she thought of his romance-inspiring sculptures. "You are a very impressive artist, Mr. Adrian. It's an honor to meet you."

He stared another second, then said, "Call me Gideon." He looked her over from head to toe. "Would you like to get away from here, Ms. Fontaine?"

This gorgeous man wanted to be alone with her? Her body screamed, "Yes!" A thrill ran up her spine at the idea. He was so sexy. He could have any woman in the room with nothing more than a grin. Her brain stepped in then with its usual mix of infuriating logic and apprehensive caution.

"Why would you leave your own party?" Lori asked, then added, "And please call me Lori."

Gideon's blue gaze turned hot, his voice rough. "Do you live here in the city, Lori?"

"Yes. I have an apartment not too far from here."

"Then I'll take you home later. First, I'd like to be alone with you. It would please me very much if you gave me the pleasure of your company. I wish to get to know you a little better. Would you like that?"

Lori nodded, her voice suddenly abandoning her. A ripple of desire had her legs shaking.

"Good. And don't worry about the party. My agent is used to me stepping out early," Gideon said, waving the thought away as if the important people and expensive catering were pointless. "She'll just chalk it up to my temperamental attitude. You know how artists can be. Did you come with someone? If so, just say the word and I'll—"

She quickly cut him off. "I did come with a friend, but she seems to have forgotten all about me." She smiled, genuinely happy for the first time all evening. "I'm all yours, Mr. Adrian. Lead the way."

Gideon leaned toward her and whispered, "A very lovely thought, Lori." Then he started walking her out of the overstuffed room, leaving her to wonder at his words. When he reached the doors to the parking lot, he stopped and turned back to face her. He moved closer, and she could smell the hot, masculine scent of him. Her pussy throbbed to life.

"I think it's fair to warn you that I'm very attracted to you."

Lori rewarded him with her own little confession. "I'm very attracted to you, too."

He lifted his hand and stroked her cheek, then murmured, "I'm glad. I'd hate this to be all one-sided."

Lori swallowed around a lump in her throat, then without another word, he led the way out of the huge elaborate party hall. They moved quickly down the large marble steps to his car. He let go of her hand while he put her into his black Jaguar, then took hold of her again after he was behind the wheel and on the road.

She liked his hand. It was big and strong. Secure. Lori glanced over at him, wondering what he was thinking. In the darkness, she swore she saw him smile. It was a feral and wicked expression, and her stomach jumped.

This was either going to be the biggest mistake of her life, or the most exciting thing she'd ever done.

Chapter Two

He'd taken her to a bar? Stranger still, Lori was actually having fun. With a man no less! That hadn't happened in a very long time. To top it off, he seemed to be somewhat enraptured by her. She wasn't sure what to make of it, or him.

They were in a little dive of a place on the other side of town. He must have been a frequent customer, because he knew the bartender by name and asked for his usual, which, as it turned out, was a light beer. She ordered the same, and they sat at a little booth. She didn't need to look around to know the patrons were staring at her. She was one of the few women in the place who wasn't wearing jeans and a T-shirt. She must have stuck out like a sore thumb in her expensive black dress. Not that it mattered, she was just glad to be out with a man who wasn't belittling her. Besides, after being alone for the past seven months, it was way past time for some excitement. She'd damn well earned it.

As Lori sipped her cold beer, she had the feeling Gideon was thinking about her, and his thoughts weren't pure in nature either. Then again, Gideon Adrian was no angel. Anyone could see that by his art.

His intense blue eyes focused on her as if she were the only person in the room. It was a thrilling notion. What would it be like to make love to someone like him? Pure heaven, no doubt.

Lori imagined a candlelit room where the only piece of furniture was an enormous cherry wood four-poster bed. They would both be nude. In his strong, callused hands, he held a leather whip and multicolored silk scarves. He'd approach the bed, she'd be sprawled out for him, and he'd use the scarves to secure her. Then he'd drag the soft leather over her skin, making her eager and nervous at the same time.

She shook her head and forced her mind back to reality. Who was she trying to kid? Her one relationship had ended up in an engagement, then one year later a break up. It'd been a mediocre relationship that had led to a bitter end. What did she know about sexual delights?

She stopped her mental musings and looked across the table, then realized she wasn't being a very good date. Gideon's gaze was warm, tender, and she wondered what he was thinking in that moment.

"So, Mr. Adrian, what made you want to leave a party being held in your honor?" She propped her head on her fist. "I should think you'd want to celebrate."

"I am celebrating. With you." He winked and Lori nearly melted. "And please, call me Gideon." He stroked his thumb across the back of her hand, the hand he still hadn't surrendered.

"So, what brought you to my party, Lori?"

He said her name like a caress, and Lori had to remind herself to breathe. She looked down at the table, mesmerized at the feel of his thumb stroking over her palm. Once more Lori wondered what it would be like to have him touching more than her hand. She blinked and looked back up at him and realized he'd asked her a question.

"Margaret, the woman I came with, insists I need to get out more. Plus, I admit I was a little curious about the man behind the statues." She felt her face heat. To hide her embarrassment she took a sip of her beer.

"Well, I'm very glad Margaret insisted," Gideon murmured. "The party was pretty boring until I saw you." Gideon's fingers drifted over the inside of her wrist, and she shivered. "Tell me, Lori, what do you think of my work?"

His manner might have been polite, but Lori had the feeling he could be very demanding. "I think what you do is very impressive. I enjoy the flowing lines and curves of your statues." She frowned, thinking of the focus of his work. "You sculpt people in such intimate positions. Why erotic art? Why not something less X-rated?" She was curious to know where he got his inspiration. His smile was intimate, and it affected her as nothing else ever had.

"It fascinates me. Men and women making love in passionate ways is a joy to create." His voice dropped an octave. "Women are interesting creatures in and of themselves. You have the joy of procreation. To bring another life into the world. I don't see it X-rated to sculpt such an extraordinary thing. Without love, without passion, where would we be? We need it, as badly as we need water. Passion is what makes us good at our job. It makes us good at what's important. To me the nude form, be it male or female, is beauty. Pure and simple. Thankfully Marie, my agent, feels the same way." Then he angled his head slightly and asked, "Do you find making love vulgar, Lori? Does the nude form put you off or is it a thing to cherish?"

She was speechless. He was so fervent about his work, so deep. She had no idea. Lori sat up a little straighter. "I find making love an intimate thing, to be shared between two people deeply in love. That love should be handled with care. Otherwise, someone invariably gets hurt."

He was quiet for a moment as if absorbing her words; then he asked, "Has someone hurt you, Lori?"

His question put her on the defensive. "Hasn't everyone been hurt a time or two? It happens. You move on."

"Yes, it happens, but that doesn't make it any less harmful." Gideon's face hardened. "You don't deserve to be hurt. You deserve to be cherished. Like my statues, you have beauty in you." He paused and then,

"I'd like to sculpt you." Lori's eyes widened, but Gideon only smiled. "Would you let me? I want to see your passion, Lori."

She was stunned. "You want me to pose? Nude?"

"I would be honored."

"Wow. I don't know what to say."

"Say yes."

She should have been appalled by the idea. She wasn't. Famous artist and sculptor Gideon Adrian wanted her to pose for his next incredible work of art. Well, she had wanted to do something to liven up her life, hadn't she? This was her chance.

"Yes," Lori rushed out. He smiled, and it made her think of a panther who'd just caught dinner. Her insides quivered.

"We'll start tonight," he announced, then rose from the booth. After placing some bills on the table, he took her hand, led her out of the bar. Then his words sank in, and she tugged him to a stop.

He turned, a frown creasing his brow. "What?"

"Tonight?"

Gideon winked. "I don't want to wait." Then he started walking again. She pulled on him once more, and he turned a questioning look her way.

"Gideon, I can't just go home with you and pose. We've only just met!"

Gideon's gaze darkened. "We may have only just met, Lori, but I felt a connection to you the minute I saw you. If you fear me, don't. I promise not to do anything to make you uncomfortable. We can go as slow as you like," he assured.

She was beginning to feel a little silly. "I'm not afraid," she avowed. "It's just that...will you want me nude? I don't think I could do that."

He reached up and stroked her cheek with the backs of his fingers, then whispered, "We won't do anything that feels wrong to you, okay?"

She should tell him they could meet sometime during the day, make an appointment for the sittings, or something along those lines. That would be the smart thing to do. The responsible thing.

"Okay."

It was out of her mouth before she could stop it. Butterflies played in her stomach. If only her mother and sister were there to see. They'd both have heart failure! Neither of them was used to their spinsterish Lori being spontaneous, or doing *anything* risky for that matter.

Gideon Adrian placed her once again inside his sexy Jag, and Lori squirmed with a rush of joy. This was bound to be one for the record books.

Chapter Three

The bronze statue stood three feet tall on a shiny black pedestal. It depicted a man and woman making love. It was reminiscent of Gideon's other works. With this one, the man was standing, and he was holding the woman in his lap. She had her legs wrapped around his waist. It was titled: Tortured Heart. Curious name for a pair of lovers.

"They're obviously in love, why the name?"

"Are they?" Gideon's brow quirked up. "Look again, Lori, and tell me what you see."

He stared at her, waiting for her answer. She looked back at the statue again.

"The woman's very tall, very thin. Painfully so. The way her hipbones protrude, it looks agonizing. And her face..." She stopped and stared at the woman's expression.

"Go on," he gently urged. "What about her face?"

"She's...sad, which seems strange to me."

"Why?"

"Shouldn't she be excited? Swept away by the sheer joy of it? And her hands." She narrowed her eyes. "They're clutching onto him, digging into his flesh. It looks like it would hurt. It's as if she's afraid he'll drop her, but he's so powerful and strong. She must be as light as air. She's making love, but..."

"But?"

"It looks like she doesn't trust him not to drop her." She looked over at Gideon. "He's giving her himself completely, but she won't even give him her trust. He's the tortured heart."

Gideon was silent. He stared at her for so long, she was afraid she had offended him. How was she to know what artists were like? Then he grinned, and she breathed a sigh of relief.

"I knew it the moment I laid eyes on you."

"What did you know?" He was making her very uncomfortable under his scrutinizing gaze.

"That you had passion," he replied simply. "You are the first person to see this sculpture for what it truly is."

Then he took her into another room.

Gideon's house was not what she would have expected of such a wealthy man. He seemed to be living below his means while everyone else struggled to live far above theirs. His home, situated well outside of Cleveland, Ohio, was set far off the road on a long, winding gravel driveway. He had total privacy.

All anyone would be able to see of it at the road was several hundred feet of trees. They hid his home like a fortress. When the car had inched closer, she was able to see his home wasn't the mansion she'd envisioned.

It was a sturdy stone and wood two-story with a three-car garage. The wood appeared to be barn siding. It was probably an expensive, treated wood. The house was enchanting with its wraparound porch and privacy. The porch swing stole her heart though. She pictured dozing there on a lazy afternoon, or even cozying up to a good book on a warm summer day.

Lori snatched herself back to the present and concentrated on not smacking into Gideon's back. His strides were much longer than hers, and she was having a hard time keeping up. He walked down a narrow hallway then turned into a room to their right. He flicked a light switch and Lori gasped.

With great cathedral ceilings and a huge wall of windows, the room was breathtaking. At least three times the size of the living room in her apartment. She fell in love with it on sight.

The only light came from a soft muted lamp on an end table. It was difficult to see details. Still, she could make out the gigantic couch situated along the far wall. How could anyone miss *that*?

She had no idea they even made couches so big. The soft, black suede cushions would swallow her up. The matching chair was nothing to sneeze at either. Then again, Lori figured a man as big as Gideon would need giant-sized furniture.

As her gaze roamed around the room, she spotted

a tall wooden stool set directly in front of an artist's easel. That's where she would pose. The floor to ceiling windows behind the easel probably gave him wonderful light during the day. Then a thought struck. He'd brought her to his studio. Relief swamped her as she realized he did indeed intend to keep things professional.

Then her eyes caught sight of something that seemed out of place. An octagon-shaped ottoman softly padded. The purple was like a splash of red on a black and white photo it stood out so much. What would he need that for? Different positions maybe?

Before she could ponder the stools uses, the room was flooded in light and a gentle, sexy music filled the air. Lori quickly forgot about the stool. When she turned, Gideon slowly shut the door. A wicked smile played at the corners of his mouth. A wild need to escape his overwhelming presence engulfed her whole being.

***

Gideon watched Lori attempt to figure out the ottoman. Since he'd had the thing designed specifically for his own needs, there was no way for her to know its real use. As he pictured Lori spread out on the soft, purple fabric, naked, waiting submissively for him to pleasure her, a fire started up in his loins. He needed to get his body under control or he'd only succeed in scaring her away. That was the last thing he wanted. If he played his cards right, he'd have her open and eager very soon. Ready for anything. He ached for her total surrender. Gideon vowed to unlock her hidden passion. Breach all her barriers. One major hurdle was her asshole ex-fiancé.

What kind of man could look at Lori Fontaine and call her frigid? She had more passion in her pinky finger than any woman he'd ever known. When they'd been in the bar, Gideon had gotten angry as he read her thoughts. While she'd replayed her last encounter with Rick-the-dick, he'd had a crazy need to find the man and tear his heart out for hurting Lori. The volatile reaction confused him.

He wasn't a particularly possessive man nor was he overly protective with the women he dated. Lori was different. She awakened an archaic and barbaric need in him to seize and conquer. Immediately, he pictured himself donning a sword and knight's armor. He'd bury the sword to the hilt in Rick's chest, snatch her up, and carry her off on his black Arabian horse. As the victor, he'd ride off to make love to his willing conquest. On the heels of that thought came another. Lori spread out on a bed, ready and waiting for him to claim her.

Gideon wondered where he could get his hands on an array of soft silky scarves. Multicolored as she'd imagined in her mind. He'd wrap them around her delicate wrists and ankles. No cherry wood four-poster, but he'd improvise. He grinned at the delicious thought.

Now all he had to do was wipe the *deer caught in the headlights* look off her face and get her to feel a tad more comfortable. He wanted to begin the sketches he'd use for the sculpture as soon as possible. He frowned. No way was Lori going nude for the pose. It was too soon. He'd have to start with something different.

Gideon moved away from the door. "Would you care for a drink?"

"Yes, please. A glass of water would be nice."

Her whispery voice slid over his body like a caress. She had no idea the affect she had on him. Between the shy glances and the inviting tone in her voice, he wanted to strip her naked and fuck her right there. Just slam her against the door and drive deeply inside her hot cunt.

To take his mind off sex, Gideon picked up the small black remote which controlled the various components in the room and pushed a button. A corner of the wall opened up to reveal his fully stocked wet bar—sturdy black and steel and his own design. Out of nowhere, another of Lori's thoughts flitted through his mind. *I wonder what else that trusty little remote can do.* Gideon stifled a grin. She had no idea the many uses for the remote control.

As he poured water for her and a jack and coke for himself, he surreptitiously watched Lori move over to the couch and sit. It swallowed her tiny figure. She looked like a child sitting on his enormous couch.

"Are you comfortable?"

She nodded. "I could drift right off in this thing."

Of course, no woman in her right mind could fall asleep while you're around. The man is so bad for a girl's peace of mind.

Gideon nearly choked. He really shouldn't read her mind, but he was no saint. As she straightened her dress and crossed her legs, he picked up their glasses and went to her. As his shadow fell across her, she looked up.

"You walk very quietly. I didn't even hear you."

"Thank you...I think," he said, then handed her the glass of water and sat next to her. They were close, but not touching. It was enough to make him want to yank her off the cushion and plop her on his lap.

As Lori peeked at him from under her lashes, he smiled. Her mind was a jumble of things. She kept wondering why she'd allowed herself to come to his hideaway. She saw herself as logical and realistic. He wanted to prove to her she could be so much more.

"So, tell me what you have in mind, Gideon. I'm not sure what you want me to do. How would you like me?" she blurted out.

Gideon sputtered on his drink. He quirked up an eyebrow. "I'd like you any way I can get you." As she started to blush and stammer, he took pity on her and explained, "But for now why don't we start slow. You can change over there."

He pointed to another corner of the room.

She frowned. "Nothing's there, just empty space."

He pushed his little black remote, and the corner itself popped away from the wall.

"That's so cool."

He grinned. "It is pretty cool. I have a friend who knows a lot about electronics. He designed it."

"What else does the remote do?"

"Lots of things," he answered mysteriously; then before she could ask further, he pointed to the room. "There's a dressing room and several outfits to choose from. Pick whatever makes you feel most at ease."

"Uh, I really am out of my element, Gideon," she said shyly. "I have no idea what I'm doing."

He took her drink out of her hand and laid it on the end table, along with his own. Gideon took her chin in his palm and drew her gaze to his. "You don't have to do a thing. Just sit and look pretty, the rest is up to me." He looked her over, and murmured, "I would like to see more skin, but you don't have to get naked." He saw her fear and was quick to reassure her. "I know you aren't comfortable enough with me yet, but I'd like you to go into the dressing room and pick whatever catches your eye. Don't think too hard. Just put it on and come out here. You'll sit on that stool there—" He indicated the tall wooden stool in front of the easel. "—and I'll begin sketching you."

Her relief was tangible. Unbidden came an image of her posed decadently across the purple octagon. Gideon's eyes widened as he realized the image had come from her mind.

Gideon showed her to the small one room dressing area. There was a rack full of silky, shiny outfits, he'd acquired over the years.

She quirked a brow at him. "Past girlfriends?"

He chuckled. "No. These are used for models only. And they're always sent out to be cleaned after each use."

"Pick what feels right to you, Lori. Take your time. I'll be ready whenever you are."

As she nodded and turned to the rack to survey the clothing, his mind saw her stripping out of the dress. Gideon had to force himself to leave her alone. Knowing she'd soon be bare, a mere few feet away wasn't helping his situation any either. As his pants became uncomfortably tight again, he wondered how he was supposed to get through the sketch.

He picked up his drink and swallowed the last of the liquid in one gulp. No doubt about it, he had a very long and uncomfortable evening to look forward to if he didn't get her past her reservations. The thought of driving her home without sampling her body first wasn't the way he wanted it to be. If he had anything to say about it, he'd spend the entire night showing her just how hot she could get. By the time morning came around, she'd know exactly what her body was capable of, and her ex-fiancé's nasty "frigid" remark would be a distant memory.

First, he had to follow through on the sketch. Then the seduction would begin.

Chapter Four

Drawn immediately to the purple gown, Lori took it off the rack and held it up. It stood out from all the blacks, reds, and whites. It was extremely revealing. Certainly nothing like her old flannels she had at home.

It had full billowy sleeves of see-through lace with a matching lace bodice. There was no back to speak of, leaving her bare to the waist. The translucent bit of purple silk was floor length, and it was beautiful. She thought of the stool. "He apparently loves the color purple."

"Well, Lori, here goes nothing."

She gave herself a pep talk as she unzipped the side of her dress and let it drop to the floor in a puddle of black, leaving her with only a black strapless bra and matching G-string panties. She took them off next. She turned and looked into the cheval mirror standing in one corner of the small dressing area and saw her bare body with all its flaws and imperfections. But Gideon had called her beautiful, and she was determined to believe him. She wanted to prove to Rick that she could be desirable. She wanted to prove it to herself.

She turned back around and slipped into the nightgown. Lastly, she took out her hair clip and let her hair simply cascade down her back. She ran her hands through it once, and she was done.

Before she could talk herself out of it, she left the safety of the dressing room and walked into Gideon's studio. Only this time, she was displaying every detail of her body, without the concealing help of the color black or the fantastic gravity-fighting bra.

Gideon saw her from across the room and began striding toward her. Lori kept her eyes to the floor in an unconsciously shy gesture, but when she felt his strong callused fingers tipping her chin upward, she took a deep breath and looked directly into his intense blue eyes.

***

"You are more beautiful than I'd ever imagined, Lori," Gideon growled as he looked her over from head to toe. Lori became more nervous than ever, but he couldn't seem to help himself; he had to get his fill.

Her breasts were full and heavy. They lay against her body, rising and falling with her quick breaths, tempting him beyond measure. They would fit perfectly in his large palms. His eyes trailed lower to her nipped in waist, then the flare of her full womanly hips and thighs. Her legs were strong and lean, not too skinny, just right for a man his size.

The purple nightgown fit as if made for her. It was nearly transparent and he could barely make out her dark brown nipples and the soft dark thatch of curls at the juncture of her thighs. He loved the way the purple seemed to caress her skin.

Finally, as Gideon walked a circle around her, inspecting her from every side, every angle, he was able to see her hair in all its glory. The honey-blonde mass fell well past her bottom. Each time she moved it teased him by sweeping across that gorgeous ass of hers. As if to say, "just look what I get to play with." Making him wish he could reach out and play too.

Lori was gifted with the most lusciously round ass he'd ever seen. Gideon allowed a smile to slip across his face, as he thought of her laying spread out on her stomach, with her hair all around her bare body wrapping him up in its web as he made love to her. He wanted to feel his cock slide down the cleft of her buttocks as he pushed slowly into her from behind.

"I want you," he growled.

She seemed to come to a decision in that moment. "I want you, too."

"You aren't afraid?"

"Yes. But I don't care."

He grinned. "You won't regret it, baby."

"I know."

Gideon took her hand and led her to the doorway

of his studio. Neither of them spoke another word until they were upstairs in his bedroom. The instant his gaze landed on her at the party, he'd wanted her in his bedroom.

"It is the most difficult thing not to take you against the door. To shove up that nightgown and play with you until you quiver and plead."

"Oh god," she groaned.

"But you need to be loved, gently, thoroughly, and I can't do that if I take you like a rutting buck. And the first time I make love to you, Lori, I assure you it won't be against an uncomfortable slab of wood."

He picked her up and laid her down on the bed, then stood back. She looked right there. As if she belonged. There was something pure and special about what he felt for Lori. He just wasn't sure what it was, and he wasn't certain he wanted to explore it too deeply right now.

"The first time we make love?" Lori repeated. "Are you saying there will be more than one time? And where will they be if not in a bed?"

Just barely, Gideon stroked the silky length of her honey-blonde mane and said, "You better believe there will be more times to come. So many in fact that you'll think it's easier just to stay in bed...waiting for me to make love to you." He moaned. "Hmm, I think I like that idea."

Lori giggled. "I just bet you do."

He lay down beside her with his head propped up on his elbow and whispered, "And where you ask? Hmm, let's see." He paused, giving the idea some thought. "Well, the first place that comes to mind is my rather large and very sturdy mahogany kitchen table. Laying you down on top of it. You on your stomach with your arms outstretched. Your hands clutching the edge, hanging on for the ride. Your sweet ass raised up in the air for me. I'd climb on top of you, ease inside of your tight pussy. Drive into you mercilessly until you come all around me." He stopped and closed his eyes. "Oh god, Lori, I've had more than a few fantasies about you."

He licked her earlobe languidly and watched her chest rise and fall in quick spasms. "The next place I could think of would be that purple stool in my studio. You couldn't know this, but I've had that stool custom-made. It has another purpose other than to look pretty." His voice lowered an octave as he asked, "Want to know what its purpose is, Lori?" As her head bobbed enthusiastically, Gideon nearly jumped on top of her, more than a little anxious to feel her beneath him.

"It has a retractable headrest, and the seat has a lever that raises it to a more comfortable angle and position, ensuring better...performance. I bet you'd look sweet as hell on my purple stool, Lori."

Gideon was on fire. Every nerve ending sizzled with life, and he hadn't even taken off her clothes. He knew that she was feeling it, too, but didn't quite know how to go about getting what she wanted. This only proved to him how inexperienced she was in the bedroom and how totally inept Rick must have been.

Gideon craved her the way a kid craved candy.

And he had a feeling she wanted to see what he looked like in the flesh, what he felt like atop her, skin-to-skin. Yet she was reluctant to move forward. Her shortage of sexual adventure was hindering her from letting go of her inhibitions.

"I've never done the things you talk about, Gideon," she admitted softly. "As a matter-of-fact, I'm so far out of my element here that I feel a little like little red riding hood in the wolf's den."

Gideon could see the worry creasing her brow and the tense way she clutched at the blanket. The very last thing he wanted was for Lori to be shy and reserved. He wanted her to let go of her insecurities, to feel free to explore him as thoroughly as he planned to explore her.

"Baby, don't you know that your inexperience isn't something that turns me off, but something that turns me on?" She frowned at him and he smiled, just barely touching her lips with his. The kiss was light and swift, but enough to elicit just the tiniest moan from her. When he raised his head, he said, "I like that I'll be the first man to take you on a table and a stool and every damned inventive place I can think of. It turns me on to know tonight will be as special to you as I know it will be to me." He gave her a moment to absorb his words. "Now I'm going to wrap my hands around you, suck on your nipples until they ache while you rise up and down until we both fly over the edge."

He cupped one breast through the soft filmy material of her gown and rubbed her nipple into a tight peak. When he heard her beg his name, he finished seducing her with his words, so he could let his body take over. "And not to mention the shower. Lathering up your soft silky body until you're all covered in some sweet smelling soap and then watching the shower spray run down your body, rinsing your breasts, your belly, all the way down to just about...here." He touched her between her thighs, rubbing her V with his index finger. Her hips arched up off the bed, and she moaned deeply. That was all he needed. All he could take.

Gideon rose to a seated position and helped Lori pull off the gown. Then he looked his fill. All that stood between him and paradise was a few inches of space. With her hair all around her shoulders and curling around one nipple, eyes half-closed with passion, lips parted slightly and swollen from his kisses, she looked like an offering.

Gideon left the bed and stripped off his clothes, then reached down with one hand and cupped the silky softness of her mound. He lay back down on top of her and pulled her close, breathing in her scent, feeling the way her heart raced out of control. It was as he was looking into her heavy-lidded eyes that Gideon asked, "Do you want me, baby?" He pushed his arousal against her thigh, proving just how badly he wanted *her*.

But when she only nodded, his voice turned harsh. "No, damn it, that's not good enough. I asked if you wanted me. I want to hear you say it, baby. I want to know what you want."

"I do want you. I want it all, please." She cried out, squirming under him.

"That's right, baby. That's a good girl." He cooed, as he leaned down, rewarding her with a light teasing kiss.

He rose back up and made her beg some more. "I want you, too, and you'll give me what I want, won't you, sweetheart?"

"Yes, Gideon. Oh, God, yes!" Lori screamed. Pleaded. Beyond caring about propriety.

The time for words was long past. He leaned his head back down to the pillowy softness of her breasts and squeezed them both with his hands, first kissing one then licking the other, relishing their fullness. He nuzzled his face in the valley between, and she whimpered. Gideon inhaled her sweet scent, deliberately driving himself mad. She was a powerful mix of heat and aroused woman.

He didn't think he could wait another second to be inside of her. He wanted to give her as much pleasure as he could. He wanted to give her something she couldn't get with any other man. If he pleased her well enough, she'd come back for more. Need more.

Gideon reached down between their bodies and caressed her tiny bud. She moaned and he watched her twist and thrash as his fingers continued their torture. He delved his middle finger into her wet opening, letting his thumb slide over her swollen clitoris. He heard her scream. Gideon couldn't believe how responsive she was. Every moan and shudder drove him higher and higher. Her pussy tightened around his finger, and he closed his eyes, reveling in the delicious torture. He ached for his cock to feel that squeeze.

"Christ, you're tight." He wasn't sure who would be the one begging by the time they were finished. Then all thought fled as she began bucking wildly beneath him. Gideon pulled his finger free of her and put his mouth to her instead, aching for a taste of her tangy juice. He licked and teased her with his tongue, and when she plunged her fingers into his hair and shouted out her climax, he nearly came with her.

He kept his mouth to her until the spasms subsided. Then he lifted up and touched his index finger to her lips. "Taste yourself for me." Gideon watched as she sucked his finger into her mouth and licked it clean. "Mmm, see how sweet you are?" Not waiting for an answer, Gideon twisted around and grabbed a condom from the bedside table, then positioned himself at her cleft and waited. His voice was a strained command. "Open your eyes. I want you watching."

Lori's eyelids fluttered open. "Don't hurt me."

Gideon heard her fear, and he saw the weariness in her eyes. He was taken aback for a second. But then it dawned. "Sweetheart, have you been with anyone since Rick?"

She shook her head, and he cursed himself for not asking sooner. He kissed her lightly then slid his tongue down her chin to her throat. He tasted her erratic pulse and felt her excitement. He made a leisurely path farther down and licked one nipple. He nipped at it and sucked it into his mouth tasting her sweet skin. But it wasn't enough. He needed to know her thoughts; he wanted to be inside her mind when he took her to heaven.

Slowly, Gideon lifted his head and spoke more gently this time. "What I'm going to do won't hurt. Do you trust me?"

In a breathless whisper, she said, "Yes, Gideon."

Gideon saw trust in her eyes, and it made him feel ten feet tall. He responded by slowly pushing into her narrow passage. "God, you feel so good. So damn hot and tight." As she shuddered, Gideon swiftly let down the wall inside his mind he'd been holding firmly in place and allowed himself the luxury of drowning on her wildly erotic thoughts.

They came at him in spasmodic and fragmented bits and pieces. He nearly exploded at the excitement Lori was feeling. He pushed a little farther into her; her pussy squeezed him beyond reason. He had to stop or he wasn't going to last. As she became accustomed to his size, she started to push her hips against his, driving him mad.

"If we don't slow down, I'm going to come," he admitted.

She devoured him with her gaze. "Isn't that the plan?"

Overcome by tenderness, Gideon leaned down and pressed his lips to her throat. "Yes, but not so soon."

"Oh."

He continued to tease her jumpy vein with his

tongue. She shuddered beneath him and moaned his name. "Are you okay?"

"You're a little bigger than average, but I'm fine."

Her voice was breathless, and it urged him on. He pushed a little farther inside, her body clenching around him like a fist. They both whimpered. "Is bigger a good thing?"

"Oh my, yes."

Her lips parted. The pink flush over her cheeks and neck spurred him on. He started moving in a sensual rhythm, sliding in and out, taking his time, filling her to the hilt. It wasn't enough, would never be enough. He rose up and hooked his arms beneath her knees and spread her wider, then thrust in hard, fast.

He never took his eyes from her, never left her mind. When her lashes started drifting down, Gideon's harsh growl, "No!" caused her to open them wide. "I want you to watch what I do to you." He gentled his tone. "I want you to know who's going to make you scream with pleasure. Once I'm done fucking you, there'll be no doubt that only I can make you feel this damn good."

**

Lori heard his words and watched the strain on his face. He was holding back, maintaining control. He was giving her gentle, but she wanted rough.

Lori wrapped her legs around his hips and arched her bottom off the bed. The motion pushed his cock inside her so far she felt impaled. She let loose a whimper of pleasure and threw her head from side to side. The feel of him buried so deep was overwhelming.

"God, baby, I'm going to lose it if you don't stop," Gideon growled.

The muscles in his neck were straining, and his sinewy arms were anchoring her to him, effectively keeping her in place, forcing her to submit. It was as Gideon reached between their bodies and caressed her clit with one talented finger, stroking her wet heat that she came undone.

Lori's eyes widened in surprise, and she shouted out his name as an explosive climax rushed over her. That was all it took. He drove into her fast and hard, pumping like a man gone mad. Then he joined her, pouring every ounce of his seed inside of her tight sheath.

They lay sweating and exhausted with Gideon still inside of her for several minutes before he finally left the bed and went to the bathroom. That's when she noticed a four inch long scar running down his right shoulder blade.

"What happened to your back?" she asked as he reentered the bedroom.

"An accident when I was a kid."

"It looks painful."

He lay down on top of her. "Not anymore"

She started to ask for details, but he spoke over her. "Why did you push me?"

"What?"

"Don't play coy. I wanted to make love, slowly, but

you didn't. Why?"

"Because you were deliberately holding back and I didn't want that."

"I wanted to pleasure you. Hell, you *deserve* to be pleasured."

"It was pleasurable." He frowned. "I may be shy, but I know what I want, Gideon, and I didn't want sweet."

"You wanted rough."

He wasn't asking, but she answered anyway. "Yes."

He slipped down her body and kissed her belly. Her body was so attuned to his touch; she came alive in an instant. As he made his way between her legs, she stiffened. "What are you doing?"

"You got what you wanted. Now, give me what I want."

He pushed her legs wide and stroked a finger over her labia.

"Gideon!"

"Hush, baby. It's time for me to play." As he slipped his tongue inside her body, she gave in and let him have his way.

She'd never once had multiple orgasms. She'd figured she wasn't capable. Apparently she'd been wrong. Who knew?

She had to hang on to him for support when his mouth leisurely licked up and down between her swollen folds.

"Gideon," she pleaded, unsure what he expected of her. When he hummed against her wet clit, wrapped his arms around her hips, and clutched her bottom, she melted. She tried to wriggle free, aching to open her thighs for him, to give him better access, but he held firm. Sinking his tongue in, he laved at her, restless, as if starved for her flavor. Tremors built inside her core when his talented mouth found her clitoris. He suckled the little bud. Lori came undone. She clutched at the sheets and held tight as she rode out another wild climax.

After she settled down, her legs weak, Gideon shifted his body so he lay next to her. He pulled her in tight. She felt cherished and protected. It'd never been that way with Rick. Usually she felt like crying. Sad because once again she'd let him down. Everything about Gideon was different.

"I love the way you shout out your pleasure." He cupped her chin and turned her toward him for a kiss. His tongue plunged deep inside her mouth, tongues touching, teasing. She tasted herself on his lips, and it made her crazy for more.

He lifted an inch and said, "I've never seen another woman let herself go the way you do. It's fucking beautiful."

Her cheeks heated. She shouldn't be shy, her mind knew that, but for some inexplicable reason she couldn't talk about sex quite as casually. Maybe it was the difference between men and women. She suspected it was the difference between a man used to having a casual fling and a woman who wasn't capable of equating sex with anyone she hadn't already handed her heart to. She didn't want to think of all that now. She wanted to enjoy the moment. After all, wasn't that the purpose of being spontaneous?

Determined not to punish herself for feeling pleasure, Lori turned away, pleased when Gideon wrapped one arm around her middle and pulled her in close so they were spoon fashion.

"This isn't casual."

Her heart nearly stopped. "What did you say?"

"I know you're probably thinking this is routine for me, but it's not. You're different. Remember that."

Butterflies flitted through her stomach at his words. "Thank you."

"For what?"

"For making this night so special."

He smoothed his palm over her stomach. "Don't start thinking I'm done with you. I've got lots more planned, sweetheart."

She giggled. "I know, you told me. The shower, the table, the stool."

"Yeah, all that and more." She felt his lips pressing into her hair. "Go to sleep, baby. I've got you."

As if he had so much command, her eyelids grew heavy. Her last thought was how good it felt to be held.

Chapter Five

Gideon got up early, aching to get to the sketch. Lori grumbled about not being a morning person, but he won her over with a hot shower that lasted far longer than he intended. Afterwards, he helped her blow dry her hair. He loved her hair. He could spend hours playing with it.

He instructed her to wear the purple gown again. At first she refused, but he eventually talked her into it. Gideon suspected it had more to do with her enjoying the way she felt when she wore it and less about his coaxing. She turned into a confident sex goddess, and it was stunning to watch the transformation from shy wallflower to vixen.

They had a quick breakfast of bagels and juice, and now he stood in his studio savoring the sight of Lori's womanly curves. He heard her thoughts inside his head as easily as if she'd spoken them aloud.

What if he finds me lacking, and he sends me on

my merry way?

He responded impulsively. "You could never be found lacking, Lori, and you're sure as hell not going anywhere." Too late, he realized he had answered a question she hadn't asked.

Her body stiffened as she grasped the enormity of what just happened. In an instant she shut down, and he could almost feel her withdrawing from him physically as well as mentally. She was leery of him now.

He cursed himself for a fool, but before he had a chance to cover his mistake, to ease her mind, the door to his studio was slung open and shut. Then it was a man's thoughts invading his mind.

Yum-yum, Gideon old buddy. What have we here?

At once, Gideon's entire body pulsated with a kind of rage he'd never before felt. Every muscle tensed, and his nostrils flared as if sensing a rival. He looked over Lori's head and saw his visitor come into the studio. As Gideon locked eyes with the newcomer, a smile spread over the man's arrogant face. On instinct, Gideon moved from behind Lori and stepped directly in front of her, using his body as a shield.

Gideon crossed his arms over his chest. "I'm busy, go away."

"Aw, Gideon, is that any way to talk to your oldest and dearest friend?"

He was being baited, but he couldn't seem to stop himself from rising to it. The idea of another man seeing Lori clad in the tiny bit of purple silk, nearly nude, made him want to smash something. That *something* was walking closer to them, closer to Lori. Gideon's fury boiled over.

"If you don't leave now, you'll be my oldest and dearest *dead* friend, Gregory."

Gregory tsked, not at all alarmed about the frenzy he was causing. "Introduce me. I know your mother raised you with proper manners." He angled his head to the side in an effort to see around Gideon's body.

"I'm not introducing you. Get out before I lose my temper and pound that pretty face you're so fucking proud of."

Lori's low husky voice stopped any reply Gregory would've made. "Uh, hello? I'm Lori Fontaine."

Apparently, her good manners overrode her shyness. Gideon groaned. "Don't bother with niceties, he's not staying."

Lori shoved him, and when that didn't get him to move, she sidled around him. Great, with him she's a shy wallflower, but with Gregory she's all smiles. To add fuel to his already out of control fury Gregory could now see her from head to toe. Gideon was forced to watch as the son-of-a-bitch got a good long look.

Gideon wanted desperately to twist his friend's dick in a knot for the vulgar thoughts running rampant inside of his depraved head. Never mind they had just been running around in *his* head as well. He was allowed to think of Lori in various sexual positions; Gregory wasn't.

Gregory moved dangerously close to Lori and

reached a hand out to her. "It's very nice to meet you, Lori Fontaine. I'm Gregory Kent." His smile was flirtatious, and his silvery-blue eyes lit with delight. The damn rascal was flirting with her.

Fuck me, Gideon. She's incredible!

Gideon stepped forward, ready to send his best friend to hell with one well placed fist, when Lori reached out as if to shake Gregory's hand. He stopped her with one hand clasped around her wrist, then gently nudged her behind him again.

"Gideon, you're embarrassing me," she muttered.

He swung around and pinned her with a furious glare. "If you don't want to see blood shed here today, then you'll stay where I put you."

Immediately he knew he'd made a mistake. She was good and pissed now. In her mind she envisioned strangling him.

"Look, you can stick your blasted easel and stool where the sun doesn't shine!"

Gideon placed a finger to her lips. "Don't forget what you're wearing right now, sweetheart. You just gave a complete stranger a free show."

Her eyes narrowed. "You may as well be a complete stranger, Gideon."

That stopped him for a moment, but then he leaned in close and whispered, "We made love last night and this morning. You screamed my name. That sure as hell changes things, baby."

A flush spread over her cheeks. Hell, he knew he was acting like a jealous lover, but he couldn't seem to stop himself. When the same thought popped into her head, it compelled him to respond. "I've never been jealous with any other woman." He spoke the words in a low tone, meant for her ears alone.

Her eyes held a thousand questions, and Gideon wanted to answer every single one of them, but first things first. Gideon deliberately raised his voice for Gregory. "Now, please stay where I put you and we'll talk after I get rid of this asshole."

"Hey, I resent that!"

A headache began to make itself known. As he rubbed his temples, Gideon turned back around and faced his best friend. Maybe his only friend.

"For the love of God, Gregory, go away. I'll call you tomorrow. We can talk then."

Gregory heaved a huge and exaggerated sigh. "Okay, okay, I know when I'm not wanted." But in his mind Gregory said, *you'd damn well better call me though. I want to know where you found this beauty. I just may give you a run for this one, old friend.*

Gideon frowned as he heard Gregory's final thought. No way in hell would he get his hands on Lori. She was his. She just didn't know it yet.

After he watched to be sure Gregory left, he turned around and faced Lori. She was standing with her arms crossed, a gesture that pushed her breasts high, and her cheeks were flushed. She'd worked herself up good, the truth of which lay in all the four letter words she was calling him inside her head.

Gideon thought she'd never looked more adorable or more fuckable.

"First of all, you don't tell me what to do, Gideon

Adrian. I'm here for one reason and one reason only; you wanted to sculpt me remember? But don't think for one minute that just because we slept together you have some kind of rights over me." When he thought it was safe to defend himself, she went on, "And how is it possible for you to know what I'm thinking? How do you know what I'm going to say before I say it?"

Her eyes darkened a fraction, turning them jade. His first thought was to give her some song and dance about seeing it written all over her face, something to the affect that she didn't hide her emotions very well. He'd never told his secret to a woman he was involved with before. But as he stared down at her, he realized he wanted to be honest with her. He wanted it all out in the open.

Gideon didn't want to think of the reason why he was willing to share such a huge part of himself with her. For the time being, the only thing that mattered was seeing her smile at him again.

"First off, I'm sorry for acting like an ass. Please, forgive me?"

"You're trying to charm me so I'll forgive you. But it won't work. I want answers or we're done here."

"Don't leave. I'm sorry I went all macho on you. I'm not sure what came over me." He pulled her hand up and placed a gentle kiss to her soft palm, then whispered, "But, you aren't just any woman, baby. I wanted you the moment I saw you. You took my breath away." He looked at her tempting body and growled. "You look beautiful, and I didn't like the idea of Gregory seeing you."

"Thank you for the compliment."

"You're welcome."

"Now, tell me how you are able to answer a question I hadn't asked."

"I'll tell you the truth. All of it. First, I need something from you."

She stepped back. "What?"

"This," he murmured, then leaned down and took her mouth with a wildness that surprised them both. He slipped his arms around her and pulled her close, then angled his head for better access. Gideon felt the connection all the way through; it'd been the same the first time he'd touched her. It was electrifying, and he never wanted to let her go.

Her body began to melt against him; her arms wrapped around his neck. Her moan set him off. He licked her lips and eased her mouth open, gently tasting her dark secrets. Suddenly she stiffened.

She pushed against him, and he forced his arms to loosen. "You sneak! You can't kiss your way out of this talk."

"I wouldn't dream of it, baby."

"Then stop trying to change the subject."

He sighed. "Let's sit down. It's a long story." He gave her his hand, all too pleased when she took it and allowed him to walk them to the couch. They sat side by side, but Lori deliberately put space between them. She was apprehensive, and until he explained everything, she would allow no further contact. She kept thinking inane thoughts, trying to free her mind of the images that had been there only moments ago.

She didn't want him eavesdropping on anymore of her private thoughts. Gideon knew what she was doing and immediately felt the loss. He only hoped she would understand.

"Would you like something to drink?" He was stalling, but he wasn't sure where to start.

"No, thank you."

With her hands clasped in her lap and her back ramrod straight, she waited for him to begin.

"All right then." He took a fortifying breath. "I'm not sure where to start, except at the beginning."

Chapter Six

"When I was eight years old, I was struck by lightning. I don't remember much about that day. One minute I was splashing through a mud puddle like any other eight-year-old boy, making a mess of myself, and the next thing I knew I was laying in a hospital bed with my mother hanging over me crying and frantic. I'd almost died the doctors said."

He paused, remembering the day as if it were yesterday. "I was able to leave the hospital about two weeks later, after a few tests showed all was normal. The only remnant of the incident was the scar you saw on my back. There was a recovery period and some pain, but nothing horrible. Kids are tough. The worst was bedtime. I'd start out on my stomach, but eventually in my sleep I'd turn over. Stung like a bitch, to be honest."

Lori laid her hand on his arm then whispered, "Gideon, I'm so sorry. It must have been terrible for you."

Her touch was like a healing balm, and her voice stroked his spine in a gentle caress. He moved out of her reach. He'd never be able to concentrate otherwise. Lori misunderstood his movement and thought he was pulling away. He'd inadvertently hurt her feelings.

"If you start touching me, I'll lose my train of thought."

She nodded and he continued. "After a month out of the hospital, I started getting headaches. Excruciating migraines no drug could fix. They were constant. My mother was beside herself with worry." He raked his fingers through his hair and said, "Somehow, and to this day I still don't know the how's and why's of it all, when the lightning struck me, it did something to my brain and nervous system. Almost immediately I started hearing voices. I was confused at first, but I soon realized I was hearing other people's thoughts. Their private feelings and emotions were as clear to me as if they'd spoken them." He looked at her, trying to judge her reaction. She was quiet, listening. He didn't delve inside her mind. This time he didn't want to know her thoughts.

"My mom noticed it the first day in the hospital. I hadn't. She told me I'd answered a question she'd never voiced. She knew something was wrong but didn't want to worry me. When she realized what I could do, she explained that it needed to be our secret. Later, she helped me learn how to block other's thoughts."

Lori frowned. "Why would she make you keep it a secret?"

"She was afraid if anyone knew what I could do, they'd want to test me. She didn't want that for her only child. She wanted me to get back to a normal life" He shrugged. "Or as normal as could be considering the circumstances."

He rose to his feet when he saw pity on Lori's face. "I don't want your pity."

He walked over to the window and looked out at the early morning. It was his favorite time of day. Everything was given a fresh face. Like a break from the constant pretense of normalcy. Mornings were the time when his mind could expand, and his creative juices roared to life.

Without turning around, he finished his story. "It feels good being able to tell someone. Sort of like unloading a burden I've carried around for the past two decades. Anyway, Mom took me out of school immediately and began to tutor me at home. Being around large crowds was difficult. In time she helped me with that, too. She taught me how to free my mind, showed me ways to put up mental walls to keep thoughts from bombing me." He turned and looked at Lori. "People think unpleasant things. They're not always good and pure. Hearing the immoral, the repulsive, and often the sadistic things people were thinking would've driven me insane over time. It took years of practice before I could be in a room of more than ten people without experiencing a throbbing headache." He took a lungful of air as he remembered his mother. "My mom was wonderful though. I never would've survived without her. It was her love and guidance that brought me peace and took me down a new path. She made me understand that I was unique, not cursed." When he realized Lori's eyes were too bright, he stiffened. Was she crying?

He walked over to the couch and crouched down in front of her. "What's this about, baby? Why the tears?" He kept his voice tender and soothing. He didn't like to see her tears.

Lori touched a finger to her own cheek and frowned when it came away wet. "I didn't realize I was crying." She looked at him with her heart in her eyes, and Gideon was lost in her tenderness. "I don't know. I guess it's just...everything. What you went through as a child." She laid a soft palm against his cheek. "You must have felt so alone, so isolated. And the way you talk about your mother, you love her very much, don't you?"

"Yes, I do. She was one-of-a-kind. She died of breast cancer two years ago, and I miss her still." He took her hand in both of his and pressed his lips to her fingertips. "But don't cry for me. It was all a long time ago. I'm an adult now. Thanks to my mom I live a very happy and relatively normal life." When she started to speak again, he stopped her. "Have I frightened you away yet?"

Her answer was so important to him, and he knew by now he could expect nothing less than complete honesty from her. "I'm not afraid of you, Gideon." She looked down at her lap. "I'll admit I'm a little uncomfortable."

Gideon attempted to wriggle back into her mind. Like a thief in the night, he wanted to see her innermost feelings. Without warning, Lori jerked away from him and jumped to her feet. She started to do a fast walk, to put distance between them. Between Gideon and her thoughts more likely. Gideon was faster. In a few strides he caught her in one long arm. She landed against him with a thud. He turned her in his arms and growled, "Why are you running?"

"Because you can't seem to stay out of my head!"

"But your thoughts are so delicious, baby."

"You have no right to—"

Gideon stopped her with a kiss, his lips hard and brutal. God, she tasted good. He swung her into his arms and carried her to the couch, then sat down with her on his lap. He was careful to hold her face in place without hurting her as he deepened the kiss. She had no choice but to submit to his will. Trapped against him, he knew Lori could feel his hard length beneath her bottom. He was painfully aroused. He sported a permanent hard on around her. She drove him to his knees with desire. She could have both hands tied behind her back, and he'd still be completely helpless. She was so delicate and fragile, but intelligent and determined. She was the perfect combination.

He coaxed her mouth open and slipped his tongue inside. Lori's whimpers tore at his control. He nipped at her lower lip; the little stinging bites had her moaning and wriggling. Gideon eased up and placed soft kisses over her cheeks and neck. He began caressing her jumpy pulse with his tongue, touching all the places he'd discovered drove her wild; then he suckled, leaving his mark behind.

Gideon lifted his head slowly. Putting a stop to the sensual assault took all his willpower. "Don't walk away from me," he commanded.

Lori stared up at him, eyes glazed over with desire.

Gideon addressed her again. "Face me head on, sweetheart. Don't run."

"I wasn't running...exactly," she pouted.

Gideon smiled with primal satisfaction. Lori wasn't the type to take commands from a man, but teaching her to take them from him was going to be a damn pleasure. "Then what would you call it?"

"Self-preservation. It's annoying when you invade my thoughts."

"I can't say I'll stay out. I like the way you think. The images floating around in that beautiful head turn me on."

"I don't know what to do with you," Lori complained. "You're entirely too arrogant. I want to smack you and kiss you at the same time."

"How about this. I'll tell you what I know about you, and if I'm wrong, I'll stay out of your head for the rest of the day. Deal?"

She smiled. "I'm all ears. Give it your best shot."

"You're always in control, always the responsible one. It's your mom and sister who are the spontaneous ones. You want someone to take the lead for a change. You'd love to let someone else make the decisions, but you don't trust anyone enough. How am I doing so far?"

She looked away. "Not too bad."

"You're going to learn a few things today, sweetheart. The first of which is that submitting to a lover doesn't make you weak-willed. Just the opposite. It takes a great deal of courage to give someone so much trust. I want to prove you can trust me."

"It's not in me to be submissive. It'll never work."

"What if I said if you don't, I'll punish you?"

He wanted desperately to hear her say it, to hear the words from her mouth. She was such a controlling woman, always striving for order, but she was tired of order. She wanted to be messy, to let some of her inhibitions go.

"I'd tell you that I won't be ordered about, not by anyone."

"Shall I show you what happens when you defy me?" Gideon whispered, his smile feral. Lori was like a pretty little moth, drifting ever closer to the heat of his flame.

Straightening her spine as if determined to stand her ground, Lori stated, "It makes no difference because I don't take orders."

Gideon quirked a mischievous brow at her. They were both enjoying this game. Without warning, he flipped her over, so she lay across his lap, rump in the air, facing the floor.

"You let me up, Gideon Adrian, right this minute!"

"Nope. I like this position. You have such a pretty little ass." She squirmed, but he held her down with his palm on her back. "I warned you not to defy me," he growled, absurdly distracted by the way she began wriggling around, then issued a quick swat to her buttocks.

She yelped. "Ow! Darn it, that hurt!"

Gideon couldn't believe he was spanking her. He'd never played D/s games with a woman before. Something about being the dominant to her submissive seemed right. His mind whirled with the possibilities.

He could practically feel her outrage, but she was also becoming aroused.

"You will let me up this instant, Gideon!"

He rubbed his hand over her bottom through the purple silk, soothing the spot he'd swatted. "Say you'll obey me," he demanded. He was mesmerized by the feel of her under his hand. "Tell me what I want to hear, Lori, and I'll let you up."

"No!"

Gideon swatted her again. This time she let out a moan. He knew he wasn't really hurting her because he could feel her mounting desire. Lori liked what he was doing. She was just too stubborn to admit it. He was going to cream in his jeans if she didn't submit soon. With her ass facing him, tempting him, he was getting painfully aroused.

"Be a good girl, sweetheart, and tell me what I want to hear."

"Yes."

"Not good enough. Yes, what?"

Lori gave him what he wanted. "Yes, I'll obey."

Her soft voice floated over his skin like satin. "Mmm, so sweet," he praised, as he stroked her ass one more time.

Gideon smiled in triumph as he helped her to her feet. She was so strong-willed; watching her give him the lead was a major turn on.

And not once had he raised the purple gown. He deserved a damned medal for that alone.

Chapter Seven

Lori was confused by Gideon and this new game, but even more confused by her own reaction. She'd never played the submissive before. Why did she enjoy it so much? She found herself wanting more. It was disconcerting that Gideon knew her better than she knew herself.

Her legs shook as she rubbed her bottom. He hadn't really used any real force because there wasn't any pain, just a little sting. She should be angry. Outraged. The emotion that had her body growing all hot and wet wasn't anger. It was raw desire. Her clitoris throbbed, and liquid heat pooled between her thighs. She was hot and ready for sex. My God, she'd never been so ready. Who would have thought boring Lori Fontaine had a penchant for the kinky?

"I would have, and you're not boring either, so quit thinking you are."

"Dang it, Gideon, stay out of my head!" She stood

in front of him, hands on her hips and chastised him. "You need to learn not to invade people's privacy." They were eye to eye, but only because he was seated. She felt more dominant.

Gideon laughed. "Dominant? Is that what you want? You want to dominate me?" He quirked his head to the side. "Well, honey, all you have to do is let me have my way with you, then you can *dominate* me all you want."

She rolled her eyes at his shameless intrusion of her thoughts. "You're doing it again. You said yourself you can block my thoughts when you want. For the love of peanut butter block them."

His eyes widened. "Are you kidding me? I would never block your thoughts. They're far too appealing. Hell, some of the things you've been thinking today have me as hard as a lead pipe."

She covered her ears and shook her head. "Okay, let's back up a minute here." Lori sat down on the couch, forgetting about her sore bottom, then instantly shot back up again. She glared at him. "My butt hurts."

All at once, Gideon appeared contrite. "Aw, baby, I'm sorry." He wrapped both arms around her middle and hugged her to him, an innocent smile on his handsome face. "Want me to kiss it and make it all better?" he murmured.

A mental picture of him on his knees, kissing her backside invaded her mind. She abruptly stomped it flat. He had her coming and going. She didn't know which way was up.

She closed her eyes and threw her arms up in the air in exasperation. "Can we please just stop and have a rational conversation like two normal adults?"

Gideon seemed to rein himself in. He was such a passionate man and so sure of himself. He knew what he wanted, and he was going after it full force. Lori wasn't quite ready. She'd never been with anyone who wanted her with so much fervor. It was a little scary. She needed breathing room.

"I'm sorry. Really, baby, sit down beside me." When she stared at him, he pleaded, "Pretty please?"

She looked at the couch in apprehension. "Just ease onto it, honey. I promise it won't hurt."

She slowly sat. He was right, it didn't hurt. In fact, her bottom wasn't sore at all. For some insane reason that rankled.

"Now, where were we? Oh yes, I was telling you all my dirty little secrets, wasn't I? So, Lori, do I frighten you now?"

She frowned. "Why should I be afraid?"

"Because I can read your mind. That would make anyone uneasy."

She answered with complete candor. "I could never be afraid of you. If I were, do you think I'd still be here?"

"No, I suppose you wouldn't." He paused, as if giving it some consideration before adding, "Most people are a little cautious around me, and they don't even know what I can do. Somehow I guess they sense something is different." He narrowed his eyes. "I'm glad you aren't afraid of me. I would have hated if you looked at me differently."

"How do I look at you?"

His grin was wicked. "As if you want to eat me up."

She tried to ignore how handsome he was when he smiled and said, "I'm only posing for you, remember? Eventually you'll have your statue, and our association will be finished."

A muscle in his jaw jumped. "Our *association* may have started out as artist to model, but it's quickly turned into something much more."

As his voice slid up and down her body, she blurted out her thoughts without thinking them through. "How do you do that, Gideon? How do you make your voice so irresistible? It makes me want to give you whatever it is you ask."

"If my voice was so mesmerizing, I'd use it to make you take off that purple silk, so I could see all of you with nothing hindering my view."

She frowned. "Uh-uh, no way." Besides, Lori knew she was terribly shy. The idea of stripping with the lights illuminating her imperfect body was not the same as making love in the softly lit bedroom the way they had the previous night.

"I'm turned-on right now too, but I'm not as open about my sexuality as you." Heck, if she took off the one thing preserving her modesty, she'd fall into his arms and do anything he asked. Lori knew he'd ask for plenty too.

"Yes, I would," he confirmed. "I want everything from you, and soon you'll not feel a need for such ludicrous modesty." Her back stiffened in annoyance at having once again been caught thinking of him.

"Stop it, Gideon. I mean it."

"Fine," he conceded. "If it makes you feel more at ease around me, I promise to stay out of your head...for now."

He could easily lie to her; tell her he wasn't slipping into her mind even while he did as he pleased. If she knew nothing else of him, she did instinctively feel he was a man of his word. If Gideon said he would block her thoughts, then she believed him.

Her lips quirked up despite her worries. "You just couldn't resist adding that last part could you?"

He smiled broadly and left the couch. "I do know my own limitations." He held out his hand and said, "Let's get this sketch out of the way. Then we can concentrate on more exciting things."

His smile was contagious and Lori relaxed. She wouldn't have to shield her mind from him. She had free rein to think all the naughty things about his sexy body she wanted. He'd be none the wiser.

She grinned shamelessly and took his hand. "Ready when you are."

Chapter Eight

Gideon perched her atop the hard wooden stool and instead of posing her, he'd insisted she sit whichever way was most comfortable. With her legs crossed and her hands in her lap, she seemed as relaxed as she was going to get.

"Turn to the side a little and give me your profile."

She moved to the right. "Is this better?"

"Perfect," he said then arranged her hair until part of it spilled down her back. She took his breath away. "I know it's difficult, but try not to fidget too much."

"How long will it take?"

He went behind his easel and started arranging things. "Not long."

"Why did you want my profile?"

"It allows me to see your curves better."

She shrugged. "You're the artist with all the millions."

He laughed. "And you're my sexy model with the

legs that could stop traffic."

She didn't respond, but the pleasure in her eyes was enough. She liked his compliments.

A few minutes passed and she said, "It seems as if I've been sitting here for hours. My knees are getting stiff. How much longer?"

Gideon tsked. "You've only been sitting for fifteen minutes, love. Have some patience."

For some reason, the use of the endearment seemed appropriate. He'd never called a woman that before. It was too intimate. Somehow it fit Lori.

Long minutes passed and Gideon was having a difficult time keeping his mind on the task. Her curves and shadows fascinated him, and she was an easy woman to sketch. To recreate such beauty with his own two hands was pure delight. But his thoughts kept straying into sexual territory.

It was obvious Lori didn't think she had sex appeal, but she was way wrong. She could make a monk sit up and take notice. With a body like hers men probably went weak in the knees all the time, she just wasn't aware of it. Her sexy cat eyes and full round breasts made his mouth water. He wasn't even going to think about her legs. Christ, they seemed to go on for miles. Legs that led up to a delicious ass.

He needed to get his mind off sex. There'd be time later for all he had in mind. As his gaze locked on hers, he realized she'd been looking him over. He was tempted to slip inside her head, but he refrained. He wasn't used to holding himself in check, and he realized he'd become spoiled with his ability to read her so easily.

"You're very focused. The room could be set ablaze and you wouldn't notice."

If she only knew how easily she'd distracted him. "You're easy to sketch, and you're being very patient. That helps my concentration a lot."

"Thank you."

Her shy response to a simple compliment made him angry. Hadn't anyone ever praised this woman? Her ex-fiancé was a fool. She deserved so much better.

Watching her now, fairly quivering with excitement, Gideon knew he'd enjoy spending days pampering her. He ached to show her what a treasure she was. As her eyes slid over his upper body, the only part of him visible, he had to wonder if she was getting as worked up as he. Were her breasts tingling at the idea of his hands paying avid attention to them instead of the sketch? Was she thinking of his fingers plying her nipples instead of a pencil? God, he badly wanted to drop the pencil.

When Lori licked her lips and fidgeted on the stool, he knew she was on edge. Hell, a man didn't have to read a woman's mind to know if she was ready and aching. When it came down to it, if it weren't for the easel hiding the lower half of his own body, she'd know just how eager he was as well. Looking at her was a delight, but it was pure hell not being able to touch.

Time to take his mind off what lay just beyond his reach.

"So, tell me more about yourself, Lori. What do

you do for a living?" Surely talking about her job was safe territory.

"I'm a teacher at Sunbury North." Lori smiled. "My students would never believe what I'm doing right now. They all see me as mundanely settled and far too serious. Ha! Wouldn't they be surprised?"

"Will you tell them?"

She shook her head. "I don't usually share too much about my private life with them."

"I never imagined you a school teacher." He thought of Mrs. Frasier again and laughed. "I went to Sunbury East, and I don't ever remember having a teacher that looked as delectable as you. Clearly, I went to the wrong Sunbury."

She laughed. "I don't think any of my students have ever called me delectable."

He stroked the graphite pencil over the canvas and said, "I would've."

"I think flirting with your teacher could get you a detention."

"It'd be worth it."

"Wait, I thought you said your mother tutored you."

"She did for awhile. By the time I was old enough to attend high school I'd learned how to put up mental shields."

"I see."

"So what do you teach?" Health class was his first thought. Oh yeah, he could easily see Lori with her come-hither eyes and voluptuous figure teaching a bunch of horny teenage boys all about the birds and the bees.

"High school accelerated English. Specifically reading and literature."

The excitement in her voice was easy enough to catch. "You obviously love what you do. I bet you're a terrific teacher. Teachers like you are rare. I hope your students appreciate you."

She shrugged. "If I've made a difference to even one student, then it's worth it."

Gideon had been so preoccupied with getting her into bed, he hadn't considered her choice of professions. Her life outside of his home hadn't seemed important. Until now. He wanted to know everything about her.

"What's the best part of teaching?"

Lori fairly lit up with enthusiasm. "Seeing them get keyed up when they learn something new is the best part of being a teacher. I knew when I was very little I'd be a teacher. There was never any doubt."

What would it be like to know exactly what you want out of life and then go for it with gusto? He'd always been unsettled. Never quite feeling complete. Sure, his art was his passion, much like teaching was for Lori, but it didn't fill him. No, there was still a part of him left wanting.

He stared—for a moment taking his mind off his work and onto the woman—and the warmth on Lori's face captivated him. A surge of pride welled up as he realized she was growing more and more comfortable around him. Gideon wanted her to let go completely. And he wanted to be the only man to witness it.

He stiffened his spine, shaking off the effect she had on him, and got back to the nearly completed sketch. The sooner he finished, the quicker he could get onto seducing the refreshingly guileless Lori Fontaine.

"I can't believe I'm about to say this, but I'm actually starting to relax even though I'm sitting here almost-nude."

"We've been intimate, sweetheart. There's no reason to feel uncomfortable."

"Aren't other women shy about posing?"

"Some. Others are more confident."

"I've never been comfortable under the spotlight."

"I understand, but I don't want you feeling awkward. Not with me. Okay?"

She nodded and he went back to the task.

"Have you been...reading my mind?"

It was so out of left field it took a second for her words to sink in. Didn't she trust him to keep his word? "I made a promise, and I don't break my promises."

She blushed. "I shouldn't have asked."

"It's fine. I admit it's not been easy, but I want you to trust me. Besides getting inside your head right now would only distract me."

"Right, got it. So, um, is this the way you normally go about creating your beautiful sculptures? I'm desperate to learn all I can of the process that brings about such wonderful artwork."

He'd always taken pride in his work, but he'd never blushed over someone's praise. Lori's admiration felt different; it was special.

Gideon shook his head. "Actually no. Normally, a customer will commission a specific piece from me." Gideon saw the intense interest in Lori's expression, and he smiled to himself. She was such a curious little thing. It was a desirable quality. She was so open and honest. He'd come across so many deceitful people, and it was refreshing to sit and talk with someone who merely spoke her mind.

Gideon kept sketching as he continued to explain the process. "I meet with them and discuss details. I need to know exactly what it is they desire and where the piece would be displayed."

One final stroke with a graphite drawing pencil and Gideon's heart nearly leaped out of his chest at the image he'd created.

"For instance, if the piece is for an intimate setting, such as a home, then the sculpture would be smaller in size, but if it's intended for a business, then it would be larger."

Gideon placed his pencil in a cup on a table next to the easel and stood back. He stared at his handiwork as he mechanically explained the final stage of the process. "After some basics are established, I give them a ballpark quote. Then a sketch soon follows. Of course, the party requesting an Adrian Original will need to understand the sketch is not a blueprint, but more a rough draft. If they like what I've drawn up, they give me a deposit and I start on the clay."

"Wow," Lori said, with a certain amount of awe in

her voice. "I had no idea so much was involved. Then her face took on a look of horror, and Lori seemed to panic. "Oh no, Gideon, I can't afford to buy a sculpture from you! Not that I wouldn't love to, of course," she quickly clarified, "it's just that I'm a teacher, and teachers do *not* make that kind of money." She bit her lip in worry. "I think somehow I've managed to give you the wrong impression."

"It's done," Gideon said, as a confident smile slowly emerged.

"It's done? Really?"

It was obvious her curiosity at what she looked like in curving lines of black and grey caused her to momentarily forget what they'd been discussing. Gideon treasured the excited interest in her tone.

"Would you like to see for yourself?"

Her eyes widened. "Could I?"

Gideon held out his hand and murmured, "Come here."

***

His hand, his deep voice, they were tempting enticements, and Lori knew she was helpless to them both. His heavy brows had bunched together while he'd worked. His confident fingers constantly, moving the pencil in slow steady strokes. Lori had been going crazy wondering what she would look like when he was through. Now, she wasn't really sure she wanted to see the way he viewed her. Still, she was curious. Would she be disappointed?

Lori stepped off the stool, stretched out her stiff legs and spine, then closed the distance between them. She became aware of the growing anticipation and tension filling her. Some of it due to seeing her picture, but most of it was because Gideon's gaze devoured her as each step brought her closer to him.

The minute Lori reached him; he grasped her hand in an unyielding hold as if he were afraid she would slip through his fingers. If she was capable of forming words, she would've told him she wasn't about to go anywhere. The hard roughness of his touch had her nearly purring. She was putty.

He pulled her directly in front of him. The entire length of his body pressed against her back. She trembled and closed her eyes. The picture was forgotten.

"Look at yourself. Open those pretty eyes and see what I see."

Gideon's deeply whispered words effectively drew her out of the web of desire he'd wound around her. She slowly opened her eyes and found herself staring at a stunningly beautiful woman. Lori was struck speechless by the alluring shadows and lines on the canvas.

"That can't be me."

"Don't be nervous, sweetheart. You are so unaware of your own appeal. How could you not know how sweet and sexy you are? I draw what I see, Lori. Nothing more, nothing less."

"It looks so…" She was at a loss for words. She didn't know how to make him understand she wasn't the ethereal beauty he'd created with his talented hands.

"It looks sensual and so damn tempting it makes me want to fuck you right here," Gideon groaned.

Lori shuddered. "Oh god."

He turned her around until she faced him. "In fact, there's the small matter of the purple stool."

She couldn't think with him so close. His scent filled her; his body turned her mind to mush. "Stool?"

He pointed to the middle of the room. She followed his finger and realized he was talking about the strangely shaped octagon she'd noticed when she'd first arrived. She had no idea why he was suddenly interested in that particular piece of furniture though. "What about it?"

"Do you remember when I told you it was custom-made?"

"Yes, but I was a little *preoccupied* at the time and not really paying attention."

"It's designed for sex."

Her gaze darted back to the stool. "It looks like a normal stool. Only bigger. I don't think I'm following you."

"How about a demonstration?"

"Uh, okay."

Gideon led her across the room to a remote control. He picked it up and took her over to the stool. As he pushed a button, one end of the stool raised up. She watched, spellbound, as he pushed another button and a headrest emerged from the other end.

"I'm still confused."

"You lay on your back with your bottom raised in the air. It provides better penetration."

Her face heated. "Oh."

"Take off your gown, baby."

It seemed taboo to make love in such a way in broad daylight. "Gideon, I don't know about this."

He bent and licked a spot behind her ear then whispered, "You'll forget about this shyness the instant my cock is inside you. All you'll feel is me, filling you."

When he put it like that, she was loath to refuse. Still there was one thing she wanted first. "Take off your clothes; then I'll do whatever you want."

"Be careful saying such things to a man like me," he warned. "I'm likely to take more than you're willing to give."

He started unbuttoning his jeans. Lori couldn't breathe. She'd just pulled the proverbial tiger by the tail.

Chapter Nine

Lori was riveted to Gideon as he slid his jeans down his muscled thighs and calves. She watched him bend and pull them off then shove them aside. Now he was naked. He hadn't bothered with underwear, and his cock jutted out, hard and pulsing. She licked her lips.

"Your turn."

Those two little words had the power to make her quiver. Lori slipped her fingers beneath the hem of the purple gown and raised it inch by inch up her legs, slowly revealing her body to him. The heat in his gaze made her more brazen than normal. When she had the nightgown just below her breasts, she let go with one hand and cupped her mound. Like him, she hadn't bothered wearing panties. Deliberately tempting him, Lori massaged her fingers over her clit. She was so wet and ready, it was hard to stay standing.

His hands came up to cup her breasts. He

squeezed and flicked his thumbs over her nipples, and Lori pushed into his palms, ready to plead for more.

"Christ, just look at you."

Her entire body revved to life at his deep voice and soft touches. "Do you like watching me, Gideon?"

"I could watch you touch yourself for hours and not get bored. Hell, I could come watching you finger fuck yourself."

His candor shocked her. "I-I wouldn't want that."

"What do you want? Tell me."

On impulse she blurted, "I want to use the stool. I want you deep inside me."

Gideon dropped his hands and ordered, "Then take off the gown, sweetheart."

She yanked the gown over her head and tossed it on the floor. His eyes feasted on her, leaving a burning path everywhere his gaze touched.

When he bent and picked up his jeans then pulled out a condom, she froze. "You had a condom in your pocket?"

"I told you last night I wanted to take you in the shower and I did. I also said I wanted to see you on my stool. Now I will."

She narrowed her eyes. "You were awfully confident."

He grinned shamelessly. "Yep."

She crossed her arms over her chest. "You aren't even aware how arrogant you sound, are you?"

He tore the foil packet and rolled the condom down his heavy erection. She couldn't look away from him. Everything he did fascinated her. He stepped toward her, took her face in his hands, and held her still for his kiss. Her knees turned to Jell-o.

"I'm not arrogant. But I do want you, and when I want something this bad, I tend to work extra hard until I get it."

She was out of her comfort zone with him. "It's never been like this."

"Like what?"

"No man has ever been so passionate with me."

"Fools, the lot of them," he growled then tugged her forward. "Sit on the stool, baby."

She eyed the massive thing, unsure and shy all over again. Gideon must have seen her nervousness and positioned her next to the stool, then gently nudged her until she was seated in the center. "Good girl. Now lay back with your head on the rest."

She shifted around until her head lay on the extended cushion, her body angled so her bottom was higher in the air. Her legs dangled over the edge.

Gideon was suddenly between her legs, his calloused palms moving over her thighs igniting her passion. He wrapped his hands around her calves and bent her legs. "Hold your legs apart."

Lori bit her lip and tried not to think of how open and vulnerable she felt. Then she did as he asked.

He dipped his head and kissed her belly then whispered against her skin, "Open yourself more. Show me you want me."

His hot breath against her flesh was all the incentive she needed. She spread her legs wide, then wrapped her fist around his cock and used it to stroke her clit and labia, before guiding him into her heat. Gideon stood up and thrust forward. She gasped.

He stilled. "Too much?"

"No, it's..." She couldn't find the words to express the sensations bombarding her. His cock touched places inside her body no man had ever reached.

"Damn, you feel incredible," he uttered as he pulled all the way out then thrust forward again.

His palms swept over her nipples, and she arched upward, seeking more of his caresses. When he smoothed his way down her ribcage and belly to play with her tiny bud, she came apart.

"Gideon!" she cried out as she flew over the edge of desire.

He thrust harder, holding onto her hips as he plunged deep. Muscles pumped and sweat glistened off his chest and abs. When he flung his head back and shouted her name, Lori wrapped her legs around him and held him to her tightly. She never wanted the moment to end. She never wanted to let him go. Suddenly it was all too much and tears flooded her eyes. She covered her face in mortification, but Gideon's gentle fingers forced her to look at him. He was so wonderful. Strong, giving and so capable. She loved so much about him. And that was the crux of it. She loved him.

"What's wrong, baby? Was I too rough?"

"No, never that. It was beautiful. You're beautiful."

He lifted her into his arms and cradled her against his chest. "You're telling me these are tears of happiness?"

She wrapped her arms around his neck and buried her face into his chest. She couldn't possibly tell him the truth. He was supposed to be a fun break from the norm. Falling in love wasn't part of the bargain.

"Yes," she mumbled, "tears of happiness."

"Look at me, sweetheart." When she lifted her head, he searched her face. Long seconds passed; then he said, "I want to slip inside your head, but I made a promise. I'll keep it if it kills me. Since I can't do that, then at least let me cook for you."

Her stomach growled at the mention of food. Okay, so she just realized she's in love with a handsome millionaire artist, but does the revelation stop her from wanting food? Nope. She sighed. "What do you have in mind?"

"I'm not a gourmet cook, but I can whip up some spaghetti and open a jar of sauce. Does that work for you?"

"It sounds wonderful."

He put her on her feet and helped her back into her mangled gown. Once she was covered, he leaned down to press his lips to her crown. Then he swatted her bottom. "Go shower and slip on one of my shirts, or I won't be able to concentrate."

She nodded and started out of the room but stopped when he called her name. She turned. He already had his pants on, unbuttoned, arms crossed over his chest. Lori didn't want to think about the devastating effect he had on her body, or she'd never make it out of the room.

"I know you won't believe this, but this thing between us is special."

"We only met last night," she reminded him, even though she felt the same way.

The distance between them prevented her from discerning his expression. "It matters little. We're both adults, and we know the difference between a casual fling and something more."

She couldn't speak past the lump in her throat. Instead, she hurried out of the room and rushed up the stairs. If she'd stayed another second, she'd be blurting out her feelings. She wasn't about to mutilate her heart by having her love tossed back at her.

As she walked into his bedroom, the memories of what they'd shared there swept through her. Sitting through lunch and pretending a casualness she didn't feel was not going to be an easy feat.

Chapter Ten

Lori was in a full-fledged panic. She'd come awake feeling sore and achy in spots she'd all but forgotten about. As she tried to adjust to the bright light streaming in through the large bedroom window, she realized two things. The first, she'd made mad passionate love to Gideon Adrian so many times she'd lost track. The second, the love filling her heart for the gorgeous man wasn't a passing fancy, and it wasn't about to go away anytime soon.

Like a coward, she slipped out of bed where Gideon lay deliciously sprawled, then tiptoed to the bathroom and stared at her own reflection. *Is that really me?* She barely recognized herself. The rosy cheeks and well-loved look was new. And she had Gideon to thank. He'd been wonderful.

She should have known she couldn't spend such a delightful time with the most perfect man she'd ever met and then walk away without a scratch. She knew herself better. She'd all but fallen in love with Gideon when she'd first set eyes on him at the party. Otherwise, she never would have given herself to him. Over and over again.

She never slept around. It wasn't her style. She'd done a good job convincing herself she was in dire need of some hot, sweaty, no-strings sex, but in the bright light of day there was no denying the obvious.

Her feelings toward him solidified when Gideon had told her about his childhood trauma. Knowing he'd never told any other woman made her heart melt. Pity hadn't moved her. The fact he'd told her about a part of himself he'd kept hidden from the rest of the world had sucked her in like a vacuum cleaner. Still, it wasn't until he'd all but taken her to heaven and back with his ardent loving on the purple stool that she'd allowed herself to fling open her soul and let him make himself at home there.

There was only one thing to do about it.

Slink away like the pathetic fool she was. Unfortunately she was butt-naked, and her clothes were still in the dressing room in Gideon's studio. Worse, she had no ride. She'd have to call her sister. Tabby would help her out of this mess. Lord knew she'd done the same thing for her more than once. After a little ribbing and giggling, her sister would gladly jump in her precious black Mustang and come to her rescue.

Getting out before Gideon woke was going to be the trick. No way could she face him. The last thing her heart needed right now was the awkward, *don't call me, I'll call you* spiel. Her stomach churned at the notion of never seeing him again. What she'd felt for Rick paled in comparison. Rick had been someone to fill the empty space, but Gideon was so much more.

Lori opened the door to the bathroom, careful not to wake Gideon, and tiptoed out of his bedroom and down the stairs. His house was big, but not so huge she couldn't find her way back to his studio. Within minutes, she'd located the remote control and opened the hidden door leading to the dressing room. Her clothes were right where she'd left them, only now they were wrinkled beyond hope. She left off the bra and slipped into her panties and dress. She grabbed up her purse and found her cell phone. Lori flipped it open and speed dialed Tabby. She answered on the first ring.

"Lori, is that you?"

She sounded sleepy and worried, and Lori knew the reason for both. "Yeah, it's me. I'm sorry I'm calling so early. I'm okay, but I need you to come pick me up." She heard her sister's sigh of relief just before she exploded into a lecture.

"Mom is so going to kill you, but not before I get my hands on you," Tabby barked. "Where on earth have you been? We've been worried sick! Margaret called here last night, wondering if I knew where you were. She said you two had gone to some party together Friday night. I wasn't worried until I realized you'd been out with that ditzy broad."

Good old responsible Lori. Never doing anything to make her family fret. It made her more than a little bit angry. Dang it, she wasn't a child anymore. There was no need to call home.

Margaret really was a ditz though; Tabby was right on that count. She hadn't even thought to wonder how Lori had gotten home until the next night?

"There wasn't anything to worry about, and I did try to call, but I couldn't get through on mom's phone, and you weren't home. I left a voicemail message, didn't you get it?"

"Snoopy must have yanked the cord out of the wall again. Mom needs to train that dog better. I did check my messages though, and you weren't on there."

"Well, I did leave a message. I'm sorry you were worried, but I'm a grown woman. I should be able to spend the weekend with a man without calling out the National Guard."

"What man?"

Tabby's voice changed from worried to curious. Lori groaned. The minutes were ticking away, and the longer she stayed on the phone the more chance of running into Gideon.

"I'm not about to kiss and tell."

She whistled. "He must be something else for *you* to toss caution to the wind."

"Look, I don't have a ride, and I need you to come pick me up. I'm at Gideon Adrian's. Do you know who I'm talking about?"

Tabby screeched. "Hell, yeah, I know who you mean. He's only the hottest millionaire bachelor on the face of the earth for crying out loud. I mean, he's always in the society pages. Man, when you decide to go buck-wild, you sure do it right."

Lori rolled her eyes at her sister's lingo and looked around the dressing area for her shoes. She spotted them under a chair. Pumps, she quickly discovered, were not at all comfortable at six in the morning. She gritted her teeth as she forced her swollen feet into the tiny bits of black leather. "You wouldn't happen to know where he lives would you?" she asked Tabby. "It was dark when he brought me here." She left out the part about being too distracted by the handsome man to pay any attention to directions.

"You're in luck because I do know where he lives. A friend of mine posed for him once, and she was just too happy to drive me by his house and brag about how great it had been."

A horrible stab of jealousy tore through her. "What friend?"

Tabby tsked. "Jealous, sis?"

Lori took a deep breath and counted to ten. "Forget I asked. Just please come and get me."

They said their goodbyes, and Lori let out a sigh of relief. She'd be back in her own apartment soon. She could whine and blubber over the loss of her heart in solitude. Oh goodie.

Lori left the dressing room and used the remote to close the hidden door. *Should she write a note?* She'd never done the note thing, but then she'd never had a one-nighter either. Err, a two-nighter actually.

She grabbed a pen and an old grocery list from the

inside of her purse, then started scribbling out an *it was great, thanks bunches* when her eyes began to fill with tears.

Well, she'd almost made it home before the waterworks started.

She swiped at her face and propped the note against the sketch he'd done of her. Lori stared at it, still shocked at the way he'd drawn her. The sketch made her feel special, but that was naïve considering he'd probably sketched hundreds of women. As she remembered Tabby's words about her friend posing for Gideon, her throat closed up. Oh yeah, she was real special.

She flung her purse over her shoulder and turned around.

Oops. Too late. The sleeping *Beast* was now fully conscious and leaning against the doorway to the studio. He'd put on a pair of black pajama bottoms, and she barely stopped herself from drooling. The gleam in his eyes had her trembling. He looked as if he wanted to give her another of his titillating spankings. Instead of feeling indignant over the idea, her body betrayed her with a rush of arousal. Drat it! Had she no self-control at all where this man was concerned?

"Damn right I'd like to spank you." He started toward her. "Going somewhere, love?"

He was back to reading her mind. She wanted to chastise him, but he looked so yummy with his dark hair all around his shoulders and his bare feet. Jesus, even his feet were sexy. She wanted to jump his bones all over again. Dang it, two nights should have held her over. She'd even been prepared to use the memories of what they'd shared to sustain her for the next fifty lonely years.

Gideon's wicked smiled told her he'd caught her thoughts. Great, just what she needed. As he made his way across the room, Lori stiffened her spine. Resisting him wasn't going to be easy, but she was determined to hang onto at least a morsel of her dignity.

***

Lori might be trying to run, but she was just as attracted to him now as she'd been last night and the night before. Gideon wasn't above using the knowledge to his advantage.

Only a few feet away now, Gideon reached out and stroked her cheek with the tips of his fingers. "Why didn't you wake me?"

She shrugged. "There was no reason to wake you."

"You don't think?"

"No, I don't," she whispered.

"You spent two nights with me. We've made love more times than I can count, and you're just going to walk away without a word?"

Her expression changed to annoyance. "Isn't that what casual is all about? No strings? No promises?"

Gideon let his fingers travel over her chin to her neck. "I thought we'd established this isn't casual."

"Did we?"

"I don't feel like letting you go, and I'm not amused by your Dear John note either."

She stepped out of his reach. "You can't tell me you want a relationship, Gideon. We only just met."

He advanced on her, but she retreated. He stopped and held out his hands. "I'm not going to hurt you so quit cowering."

"I'm not cowering," she muttered.

"You're acting as if I bite."

"When you touch me, I can't think straight."

"Fine, I won't touch you."

"And stay out of my head. You did promise."

"That was yesterday. The statute of limitations is up."

She rolled her eyes. "Don't be ridiculous."

"I won't let you walk out of my life. Not without a fight." This time when he moved forward, she didn't try to evade him. He kept his hands at his sides and growled, "Fair warning, love, I fight dirty."

She crossed her arms over her chest, making Gideon aware she wasn't wearing a bra. Christ, trying to hide breasts as bountiful as hers was an act in futility.

"Too late, Tarzan, I already called my sister."

She addressed him as if he were an unruly student, which only served to turn him on. Every little thing she did turned him on. "Then she'll be disappointed she made the trip for nothing because you aren't leaving."

"Good gravy, you can't just decide to keep me, Gideon. I'm not one of your statues."

Gideon shook his head. "*Good gravy?* For an English teacher you sure do have a rather unique vocabulary."

She edged back the slightest bit. She was aroused. He'd been in a constant state of readiness since he'd seen her.

"I'm forever trying to come up with ways to keep from cursing. I wouldn't make a very good role-model for my students if I'm cursing left and right, now would I? Although, you make it difficult, I'll admit."

"Don't leave," he murmured.

She started to protest, but Gideon stopped her with his finger to her open lips. He leaned down and cupped her chin in the palm of his hand, then pressed his mouth to hers, savoring her tiny whimpers. He licked the soft plumpness of her lips and drifted his hand down to cup her breast. She shuddered and he was lost. Gideon was edgy and restless. He wanted to devour, to take what he wanted. To make her scream in pleasure and pray it'd be enough to keep her with him.

His tongue delved into her mouth and played with hers, teasing and tempting, driving them both mad. He heard something drop to the floor; then Lori flung her arms around his neck and pulled him closer, pushing against him in a desperate bid for more.

One taste, one touch, and Gideon was on fire. What was wrong with him? Suddenly it was clear as day. Being with Lori had made him feel whole. She turned his cold house into a home. He'd never wanted a woman living with him, but he could easily imagine it with Lori. Waking her every morning with kisses, listening to her talk about her day in the evenings. He wanted it all, and he was going to start by driving her exquisite body wild with pleasure. He wanted to see her jade green eyes drift closed in dreamy satisfaction. Knowing what her wrinkled dress concealed was too much temptation to ignore.

He was determined to prove to her the difference between the tepid, half-hearted relationship she'd had with Rick-the-dick, and the hot, soul-deep relationship they could share if she only gave him a chance.

Afterwards, if she still wanted to leave, he'd have to find a way to let her go.

Chapter Eleven

Lori pulled back, breathless, chest heaving. "I-I can't do this, Gideon."

"Yes. You can, dammit." He let her pull away, but only because he had other plans. Stealing kisses was exciting, but if he wanted to drive her mindless with pleasure, it would take more than locking lips.

Gideon looked down at her bent head and knew her mind was in turmoil. He could only guess at that because she was trying hard to block him. It infuriated him even as he admired the strength of her will. She wasn't a woman he could control and dominate, not unless it was what she wanted.

Gideon titled her head back and forced her to look at him. "You can't tell me you don't want me," he said gently. "I won't believe you. Even with you blocking me out, I can see it in the way your body responds to me." He held her gaze as he slowly lowered himself to his knees in front of her. Her eyes rounded, and there was a fire he hadn't seen in them. "Before you leave I want one last taste." She started to protest. He could see the way her cheeks bloomed pink at his erotic words. In the bright light of day, she was becoming embarrassed and overwhelmed all over again.

"You wouldn't deny me this last request, would you, love?" Gideon grabbed handfuls of her dress and tugged it upward, slowly exposing the lower half of her body. She licked her lips and moaned his name. With her lower half uncovered, he could see her black satin panties. They were delicate and feminine, like her, but they were in his way. He took hold of them in both hands and yanked, easily tearing them in two. Lori yelped.

"I'll buy a new pair," he promised. "Hell, fifty new pair."

Gideon tossed them aside and stared at her glistening mound. Her soft curls were damp with arousal. He was suddenly starved for her.

"You're so goddamn sexy. Sexy and wet and ready."

"Oh, Gideon."

The need in her quivery voice urged him on. "Put your leg over my shoulder, baby."

She was unsteady but eager as she did as Gideon instructed. The position put the apex of her thighs directly into his face. It was a major turn-on. She looked a little bit awkward and wobbly in her pumps. Gideon grasped her hips and pulled her to him. He kissed her clit then growled, "I want your juice on my tongue before you leave. I want it there forever."

Gideon spread her open with his thumbs and exposed her. He leaned in and licked her slit, then his tongue moved inside her body, and his hands clasped onto her bottom bringing her closer. Gideon was swept away on a sea of desire as emotions rocked his body and tore at his heart and soul. He delved deeper, his cock throbbing as he felt her inner muscles clench around him. Lori raked her fingers through his hair and clutched onto him. She moaned as he flicked his tongue over and around her clit, time after time, until her thighs started to quiver and her body began to spasm out of control. Without warning, Lori shuddered and screamed as she came into Gideon's hungry mouth.

She all but slumped over him, and he relished the feel of soft curves, totally replete, leaning on him for support. She was vulnerable and trusting, and it pulled at him. He gently kissed her swollen nub one more time, then pushed her away just enough so he could stand. He was careful to keep a hold on her as he stared at her quick breathing and heavy-lidded eyes. Christ, he wanted to have this with her every morning. To see her smile in just such a way, just for him. It would be more than enough to make him a happy man.

"God, you do fight dirty."

The words were so unexpected and Gideon laughed. "I did warn you."

Her lips tilted up and his stomach jumped. What was she thinking? He still couldn't see into her thoughts; the brick wall she'd erected was firmly in place. He didn't have to wait long to find out what had put the twinkle in her eye though.

"Yes, Gideon, you did warn me, but two can play at that game." She tugged her dress back down and lowered herself to the floor. God, he'd never survive it.

"Uh, didn't you say your sister would be here soon?" Maybe she'd get lost on the way. It was a wishful thought, but he sure as hell didn't want anyone interrupting what she was about to do.

"Yes, but it didn't stop you, did it? You did what you wanted anyway. Now, it's my turn. I want your taste. I want it on my tongue, and I want it there forever, Gideon."

"Christ," he groaned. He loved the way this woman's mind worked. With her silky mass of tangled honey hair drifting down her back and those big green eyes smiling up at him, Gideon knew the truth. He was in love with her. He'd never in his life felt the emotion, but he was no fool.

She looked at him with a sexy wink then started to divest him of his pajama bottoms. He helped her push them down his hips until they pooled at his feet. He was about to step out of them, but she delved in before he had the chance. The first tentative touch of her lips to the bulbous tip had Gideon realizing she was a novice. She wasn't sure what she was doing, and some primitive part of him loved her inexperience. He put his hands on her head and directed her onto his waiting shaft.

"Just relax, love. Close your eyes and feel me with your tongue, your soft lips, and that sexy mouth of yours." At first, she seemed to freeze up, but then she let her eyes close, and Gideon felt a soft sigh drift over his cock. With one hand, Lori guided him inside the wet heat of her mouth, then farther until he was practically down her throat. She licked and teased. The little movements of her tongue and lips drove him mad. He tried once more to slip inside her head, and this time he found her open, probably because she was too wrapped up in what she was doing to bother keeping up the wall. Her emotions slammed into his mind strong and true, not fleeting as she'd pretended. She cared for him. He wanted to shout to the heavens, but her thoughts as she marveled over the intensity of having his cock inside her mouth fried his circuits. She liked his taste, his scent; she enjoyed making him crazy in this way. It made him nuts knowing she was taking delight in what she was doing to him.

Silent as a cat, Gideon pulled back out of her head and watched her. Lori was on her knees, her shyness all but a distant memory. She was beginning to find a rhythm, pulling his rigid length all the way out, placing a gentle kiss or a small lick to the tip, then sucking him in again. She was in no hurry to finish, as if she had all day to kneel in front of him and lick at her leisure. Damn he wished she could, but her sister would be there soon, and it was either finish or they'd be rudely interrupted. As she cupped his balls in her other hand and squeezed, every thought fled as his mind turned to Lori and her talented mouth and fingers.

"Christ, Lori," he growled as he grabbed up

fistfuls of her hair.

"Yeah, I know the feeling," she whispered and then her movements turned rapid, as she became more excited to please him, to taste his come. She wanted him to lose control. She sucked and licked, and suddenly he was there, flying over some unseen edge and groaning her name in feral ecstasy.

Long seconds passed, and Gideon realized Lori was still on her knees, only now she was staring up at him with her heart in her eyes. She was more beautiful than ever. He wanted it to last forever.

The doorbell rang.

Lori's eyes grew big, and her mouth dropped open. He helped her up, and she frantically went about righting her dress and fixing her hair while he righted himself. The bell rang again, and she all but jumped. When she started to sprint from the room, Gideon had to grab her from behind to stop her. "Where do you think you're going?"

"That's my sister! What if she can tell what we've been doing?" Her face turned crimson and as if by magic her shyness was back full-force.

Gideon wanted to laugh. She was so mussed only a blind man would be oblivious to what they'd been doing. "Love, what we just did wasn't shameful. It was perfect and right, and nothing is going to change that."

She wrung her fingers together in worry.

He sighed. There was no reasoning with her as long as her sister stood on the other side of his front door. He took her by the hand, linking their fingers.

"Come on. Let's go greet your sister."

She stopped him. "I hadn't meant for you to have to deal with all this," she said. "I'm so sorry. Really, it wasn't supposed to happen this way."

He frowned at her words. "What wasn't supposed to happen?"

Lori wouldn't quite meet his gaze. "I know you would've liked this to be uncomplicated, and meeting my sister is about as complicated as it gets."

Ah, now he was getting the gist of it. "Have I given you the impression that I think of you as a good fuck?" His eyes narrowed on her. "Is that all I was to *you*?"

Her lips thinned in anger. "I wouldn't have put it in such a crude way." She tried to pry her fingers out of his, but he wouldn't allow her to pull away from him.

He leaned down until they were nose to nose and he whispered, "You're way more to me than a good time." Then the doorbell rang again and Lori jumped. Gideon sighed.

"If we don't answer the door, I'm afraid your sister will only beat it down," Gideon muttered.

Lori nodded, and together they left the studio.

Chapter Twelve

By the time they'd reached the front door, Lori's sister had resorted to banging her fist against the door. Gideon pulled Lori into his side, wrapped his arm around her waist, then swung the door wide. He stopped cold. His heart nearly stopped at the sight that greeted him. The woman on the other side was Lori. Only it wasn't Lori because she was next to him.

"What have you done to my sister?" The look alike growled.

Gideon looked at Lori and rumbled, "A twin? Damn, you could have warned me. I nearly had a heart attack." Then he heard a moan, like an animal in pain, and Gideon peered around the side of the door and saw Gregory curled up in a ball cupping his crotch on the floor of his porch.

Gideon quirked an eyebrow at Lori's twin. "What'd you do to my friend?"

She looked down at the moaning mass of blond

hair. "He said something about how hot I looked in see-thru purple. Since I'd never met him before, I figured he was talking about Lori. The comment seemed entirely inappropriate, so I kicked him."

Gideon was about to thank her, but he never got the chance because she kept right on going. "Since you're the hottie Lori hooked up with, I figured you wouldn't mind so much if I kicked one of your friends in the balls, seeing as how he was blatantly hitting on your babe and all. Know what I mean?" She popped her gum and waited.

Hottie? Gideon was dumbfounded at how completely different two sisters could be. Identical in looks, but that's where the similarities ended. Lori was conservative and demure, but her twin was an unrestrained bundle of electricity in leather pants.

"Tabby, allow me to introduce you to Gideon Adrian." Lori glanced to the right of the door and added, "And the man you turned into mush would be his best friend, Gregory Kent."

Tabby had the good sense to look contrite; even if it wasn't the emotion she was feeling at the moment. "Sorry about the kick, Gregory, but you really should learn to control your mouth."

Gregory slowly rose to his feet, careful to keep his eyes both on the evil twin and on Gideon. Smart of him, Gideon thought, considering he was ready to kick his ass for flirting with Lori. Or, the woman he thought was Lori. Christ, he was getting a headache.

"Yeah, you sound sorry," Gregory mumbled then winced as he attempted to stand up straight. "I would say it was nice to meet you, but..." Gregory let the thought trail off. Gideon knew it'd be a damn cold day before Gregory ever got within ten feet of the little hellcat.

"Tabby, it's nice to meet you," Gideon said. As he kept his arm firmly wrapped around Lori, he gestured for Tabby to enter. "And I apologize for my friend. If I know Gregory, he was only flirting with you because he knew it would piss me off."

Tabby and Lori both appeared flabbergasted. Tabby asked, "He purposely tries to piss you off, does he?"

"He razzes me. It's all harmless fun."

Tabby seemed unconvinced, but Lori only smiled. She'd already had a taste of Gregory's flirtatious nature.

"So, what took you two so long to get to the door?" Tabby's gaze twinkled with mischief.

"We were busy and don't ask rude questions," Lori admonished.

Gideon wasn't about to let the opportunity pass to plead his case. "To be honest, I was just about to tell your stubborn sister here that I love her and want to spend the rest of my life with her."

Gideon looked at Lori. Her eyes were wide, and her mouth hung open. For the first time in a very long time he felt real fear. This woman had his heart in her hands. What she did with it was up to her. All he could do was wait and hope. It was damned humbling for a man who thought he'd had life all figured out.

"You two only just met!" Tabby howled.

"Does it matter?" he whispered as he kept his gaze on Lori.

"I suppose not," Tabby admitted. "So, do you love him, sis?"

More than ever, Gideon knew Lori wanted to crawl into a hole, but she mustered up her nerve and looked at her sister. "I swear, Tabby, mom should have taken away your Lady Georgina novels, locked you in your room, and thrown away the key."

"I'm not the one swearing undying love after a weekend of frivolity."

Lori shook her head, missing the look of surprise on Gideon's face and the sudden awareness on Gregory's at the mention of Lady Georgina. No one knew Lady Georgina wasn't really a lady, but a man and Gideon's best friend Gregory.

When Lori turned to him, Gideon forgot all about the mention of erotica. He nearly lost his nerve when he saw the way she bit awkwardly at her bottom lip and the uncertainty in her eyes. It made him want to hold her, to tell her it would all work out. But he held back and gave her time to say what she needed to say. He only hoped he was man enough to take it.

"Gideon, I need to be honest with you."

His entire body stiffened with those words. If she didn't get on with it, he'd be on his knees begging, and that was the last thing either of them wanted.

"I had every intention of leaving here this morning and never seeing you again. I wanted to keep this casual and light. This is the first time I've ever done anything...adventurous. I'm the one people call if they need a ride after partying all night." She paused then added, "I thought what I had with Rick was my big, once in a lifetime, love. When he dumped me, I didn't think I could ever go through that again. I didn't want to fall in love. I didn't want a relationship for that matter. But then you came along and all my plans flew right out the window."

"I'm not Rick-the-dick, love. He was a damned fool." Gideon heard snickering in the background, but he wasn't deterred. "I would never, *could* never, treat you in such a way," Gideon vowed. He took Lori's hand and brought it to his mouth. He kissed her palm, relishing her and wishing he could erase Rick from her memory for all time.

He felt a shudder run through Lori as his lips smoothed over her delicate knuckles. "No, I know you wouldn't treat me the way he did," she whispered, her desire building by slow degrees. "What I'm trying to say is that what I felt for Rick, well, it wasn't love." She gazed up at him with an intimate tenderness meant for him alone. "It was a cold substitute. I know the difference now because what I feel for you, this hot, all consuming intensity, is so much more than anything I'd known. You're my biggest adventure ever, Gideon, and I'm not giving you up. Not for anything."

Gideon couldn't believe what he was hearing, but he desperately needed to be certain she was truly over Rick. Rick had really hurt her, and he didn't want her on the rebound. "Then let me in, Lori. Stop blocking me. Give me that, right now, at this moment."

Lori burst out laughing. "You'll do anything to get

through my wall, won't you?" He only stood arrogantly staring at her, neither confirming nor denying. "I will let you in, but let this be a lesson to you, Gideon Adrian," she censured. "From now on don't force your way in, or the wall goes back up."

Now he understood. He had, in his usual cocky way, tried to wriggle his way into her head. To read her mind and see if she loved him, before he put his own heart on the line. She must've had some idea he would try to sneak in, so the teacher had erected the wall as a lesson in privacy. No one had so effectively kept her thoughts hidden the way she had. In his opinion, it was a sign they were meant to be together. Gideon grinned full out now, thinking of how damned interesting his life with her would be.

He grabbed her by the shoulders and kissed her hard. She reciprocated and opened up to him in every way. Soon they'd forgotten they had an audience.

"I have no idea what you two are talking about with all this wall business, but does this mean I'm no longer needed?"

Gideon let his lips drift away from Lori's and looked at Tabby and Gregory. "Go away you two. I've got a woman to *sculpt*."

Within seconds they were alone and naked. When he swung her into his arms and carried her to the studio, Lori said, "You weren't serious about the sculpture, were you?"

He shook his head. "Later for that. For now, I want you on that purple stool again."

She grinned and kissed his chest. "I love the way

you think." As a thought occurred, her brows scrunched up. "What do you plan to do with the sculpture once it's finished?"

"Keep it."

That surprised her. "But why?"

"There's no way I could ever let someone else have what's *mine*."

Her insides quivered. "I don't know what to say."

"Don't say anything, love, just feel."

And she did.

Epilogue

Eighteen months later...

"I realize you think I'm terrific, but you are somewhat biased, Gideon. Your agent isn't going to be swayed by love everlasting. She'll see all my flaws and idiosyncrasies right off the bat."

Gideon rubbed his forehead and sighed. "Love, you've talked to her for thousands of hours on the phone. Christ, you email each other every single day. What's there to be nervous about?"

He just didn't get it. Of course, he was a man. What did she expect? Lori unsnapped the seatbelt and inhaled hoping to calm her jitters, but it would take way more than a deep breath to quell her fears and reservations. Today was the big day she would finally come face-to-face with Gideon's larger than life agent.

What's there to be nervous about?" she shouted, nearly hysterical with the mere thought of getting out of the car. "I am about to meet the woman who single-handedly made you a sensation in the art world. She's smart, savvy, elegant, and I'm not." Gideon tried to interject, but she was well beyond soothing. "And, to top it off I look like a beached-whale!"

Gideon grinned. The dolt. She smacked him in the chest, and his grin grew. He grabbed her hand when she tried to hit him again and even managed to twine their fingers together. She had to admit, the gesture went a long way to calming her nerves.

"Baby, you are prettier and smarter than any woman on earth. If anyone should be nervous, it should be me because all the men in there are going to be eyeing you." He bent toward her and kissed her cheek. He moved a little lower, sweeping his lips over hers. Her head swam. When he leaned back, his eyes were intense and hot with passion. Gideon's voice was hoarse and edgy when he placed his palm over her belly and stared at its roundness. "And you do not look like a beached-whale. You're barely showing, love."

She gave him her patented skeptical arched-brow, but he ignored her, as usual.

"You look like the beautiful mother of my child. It's enough to make me want to tear out of this parking lot and find the nearest hotel room."

She smiled as she reached up and laid her fingers against Gideon's unshaven cheek. Suddenly she felt euphoric with marital bliss. "I only want to make you proud. This is a big part of your life, Gideon."

"True, but have a little faith." He winked, and

said, "I swear everyone in that room will love you, including Marie."

Lori's lips quirked up sideways. She was still unconvinced, but she did feel slightly less insecure. "Thank you, Gideon."

His smile was outrageous as he opened the car door on their new, and much more sensible, four-door sedan. The instant she'd announced she was pregnant Gideon had started baby proofing everything. Which included buying a safer car. Now they only took the Jag on slow Sunday drives. Since she was at the end of her first trimester, it sat collecting dust in their garage most of the time. It just wasn't worth trying to get in and out of it at this stage.

"Come on, we'd better get a move on. The sooner we get in there, the sooner I can get you back to the hotel."

"Don't even start, Gideon."

He laughed, slammed the car door, and jogged over to her side. He helped her out, ever mindful of her pregnancy. Lori batted his hands away and admonished, "Stop that, they'll think I'm some silly fragile thing who has to be coddled."

"You are fragile, and I love coddling you," he whispered then placed a quick peck on the top of her head. She wanted to scoff, but she was too busy swooning at his attentiveness. Then, as she preceded him up to the large building where Gideon's agent had booked his latest showing, she could have sworn she felt him watching her. His next words confirmed it.

"I swear your hair's grown another foot since you

found out about the baby."

"Prenatal vitamins. They work wonders."

As she approached the double doors, she felt his lips against her ear and his breath coming in pants. "That's not the only thing that's grown, baby."

Immediately she felt her breasts tingle, as if his voice had so much power over her body. Just as she was about to tell him to behave, the door was flung open, and a woman stood on the other side, grinning from ear to ear.

"Gideon, for heaven's sake let the girl breathe."

Lori immediately recognized Marie Gleason from all the photos she'd received in emails. She was in her sixties but could easily pass for much younger. With her petite, toned figure and straight, proud shoulders and vibrant blue eyes, Lori felt herself forgetting she'd had numerous conversations with the woman. She was the only other woman in Gideon's life, and Lori desperately wanted to impress her.

It didn't take Marie a second to pull Lori into a tight hug. When she finally let her up for air, she exclaimed, "Lori, I've been absolutely dying to meet you in person. Even though I feel I already know you since we've talked so much on the phone." She directed her watery eyes to Gideon and then back at her, saying, "Ever since Gideon told me he'd found the one, I knew you'd be special." She looked her up and down, and her eyes grew mistier. "I'm so sorry I couldn't come for the wedding."

Lori found her voice when Marie's last words sank in. "Oh, nonsense. I'm just glad your ankle is better."

It had given them both a terrible scare when Marie had fallen off her bicycle and broken her ankle. As a result, she'd been wheelchair bound for weeks afterwards, then on crutches for several more weeks. Marie had been crushed when she couldn't attend their very impromptu wedding.

Lori had wanted the whole white dress and huge guest list type wedding when she'd imagined herself marrying Rick. This time around she only wanted Gideon. They'd kept it a simple affair with just their closest friends and family. Lori's mom and sister, Gregory, and a handful of Gideon's art pals had attended. Gideon had won over her mother in a heartbeat.

As they walked into the huge room which displayed Gideon's sculptures, one face leaped out at her. Rick. What on earth was he doing at an art showing?

As if sensing her, his head swung around, and their gazes locked. Lori felt Gideon stiffen and pull her in close. She looked up at him and smiled. "He's old news, Gideon. We don't have to worry about him."

A muscle in Gideon's jaw twitched. "I should kill him for the way he treated you."

"No. He's not worth the trouble."

"He's right," another voice interjected. When she swung her head around, Rick was standing in front of her, eyes full of remorse.

"What did you say?"

"Your husband is right. I was a jerk, Lori, and I'm sorry."

She couldn't believe her ears. Rick had never apologized. Only accused. "Why so humble all of a sudden, Rick?"

"I'm curious about that myself," Gideon ground out.

"I had a run in with an eighteen wheeler. Made me see things a little differently."

Lori could see the change in him. He was thinner and walked with a slight limp, and his arrogance was gone. Still, there was one thing left unexplained. "I never would have taken you for an art lover."

Rick shrugged. "I'm trying new things. I'm here with a friend." He turned and motioned a handsome African American man forward. When their fingers intertwined, Lori's jaw nearly dropped. "I'd like you to meet, Paul."

By rote, Lori held out her hand, surprised when Paul smiled and took it. "I've heard wonderful things about you, Lori."

"Uh, it's nice to meet you too."

Rick smiled up at Paul then winked at Lori. "Paul was my nurse in the hospital after the accident. We've been together since."

"I see," she said, even though she really didn't. After all, what was a woman supposed to say when she finds out her ex has turned to the other side?

As they walked away, she heard Gideon snicker. She glared up at him. "Don't even say it."

"Sorry, love, it's just sort of funny."

"What is?"

"The effect you have on men."

It took all her willpower not to laugh. "I'm actually happy for him. And a lot of things make more sense now."

Gideon stroked a hand over her lower back, immediately easing the aches and pains. "What things?"

"He was never happy with me. As I think back, I'm convinced he was denying his true feelings."

They both watched as Paul leaned down and whispered something into Rick's ear. Rick smiled. "Well, he's not anymore."

"No, he's not. Seems everyone got what they wanted out of the deal."

"Yeah, it does," Gideon murmured.

When their gazes locked, Lori's heart soared. She owed Margaret big time for insisting she go to that party. Tomorrow she'd send her a box of chocolates. Tonight, she had other plans.

Lori opened her mind and brought up an image of washing Gideon very thoroughly from head to toe.

Gideon's eyes narrowed as he leaned close to whisper, "You're playing with fire."

She licked her lips and said, "Too much caution is boring."

"Mmm, I couldn't agree more, baby."

They lasted two hours before managing to slip out a backdoor.

About the Author

Anne lives in a small town way out in the middle of no-where-ville. She is a gorgeous blonde with wonderful curves and a money tree in the backyard. She never wants for anything and she always loves everyone.

You can read blurbs and excerpts of all Anne's stories by visiting her website http://annerainey.com

Chat with Anne on her Yahoo! Group
http://groups.yahoo.com/group/rb_afterdark/

Or join her newsletter to get monthly updates on all her books
http://groups.yahoo.com/group/annerainey/

TEASE Dark Tarot

Trenton's Terms

KELLEY NYRAE

TEASE PUBLISHING
www.teasepublishingllc.com

To my close friend, and fantastic writer, Anne Rainey. Thank you for being there when I need to vent and for sharing your knowledge so freely. I'm so happy to share this journey with you.

Acknowledgment

Thank you to Tempest and my sister Jessica for your Tarot help. I really appreciate it. Big thanks also to Amy, the worlds best critique partner!

Prologue

"Sid, come in here a sec." Abby held her tarot cards nervously while shuffling the deck. She'd given Sidney countless readings in the past. Hell, readings were her thing, they were what she did. So, why was she so nervous about this one?

It had to be something major. The overwhelming urge to read her best friend's cards came on too strong, too sudden for it to mean anything else. She only hoped it would be something good. It *had* to be something good. Sid deserved it.

"What's up?" Sidney asked walking into Abby's dining room, joining her at the table.

"Shuffle." Abby handed the cards to her friend. "You need a reading." She didn't mix words. Never had. Luckily she had a friend like Sidney who knew that about her and loved her for it.

Without questioning her, Sid started shuffling the deck while Abby sat watching. She was eager to see what would come up. A few shuffles later she stopped, handing the cards back to her.

"I think we can do a simple three card layout. There's something you need to know I just don't know what it is."

A nervous glimmer sparked in Sid's eyes but Abby ignored it laying three cards on the table signifying past, present and future. The past card was completely ignored. Neither woman could take their eyes off the present day and future cards: The Emperor and The Lovers.

Abby watched the look on her friend's face pass through fear before landing in a zone that made Abby want to laugh and cry at the same time. Fear and confusion shown in her eyes, but Abby wasn't worried. Suddenly, she had a much clearer picture of what lay in her best friend's future.

"Looks like someone new will be making their way into your life, Sid. You better get ready, girl. You're in for the ride of your life."

Chapter One

The Hotel lounge started to clear out while Sidney Clark sat nursing her ice water. Her best friend Abby left hours before to go out with a few of their friends from the psychic fair. For some reason she hadn't felt like going out with the girls. It didn't feel right. The quietness of the lounge called her name after the hectic day they'd had and she had to listen.

The psychic fairs were always great for business. Sidney packed up some of the books, crystals, and other knickknacks she sold in her shop, The Mystic Boutique, while Abby brought along her Tarot cards and reading table. They piled in Abby's old mini van and made the four hour drive up to Portland. Even though it was only for a weekend they always had a blast. Abby gave her readings while Sidney sold odds and ends to the shoppers.

After their day at the fair they always spent the night on the town taking advantage of the clubs and hot spots the city had to offer. Things that just weren't a part of the small town life they lived in River City. Today, for the first time since they'd started driving up for the psychic fairs, Sidney didn't go out. She couldn't say why, but for some reason she couldn't make herself leave the lounge for anything.

Now here it was ten-thirty PM and she was still nursing an ice water alone. *Maybe I should have gone out with everyone else.* Twirling her blonde curls around her finger Sidney glanced toward the door contemplating heading up to her room. All thoughts stopped as a gorgeous, raven-haired god walked into the lounge.

He was the most beautiful man she'd ever seen. His hair was trimmed short around the most chiseled facial features of any man to ever cross her path. The man was tall, standing about six foot three inches. He wore black slacks and a white button up shirt. His tie was loose around his neck with the sleeves on his shirt rolled up to his elbows.

He so wasn't her type but for the life of her she couldn't look away. He stood there like he owned the place. Strength and confidence rolled off him in waves she could almost see, but definitely felt. Whoever this man was, he commanded attention. There was only a small amount of people still littering the lounge but they'd all noticed when he walked into the room, their eyes locked on him.

Sidney felt herself become dizzy. Realizing she held her breath she let the air release from her lungs slowly before reaching for her glass to take a drink. As she set the glass down on the table her mystery man glanced toward her, his ice blue eyes locking on hers intensely. Without so much as a second thought he ambled toward her in long, quick, determined strides.

Oh God, it's him. She knew it before he reached her table. This was the Emperor Abby warned her about in her last reading.

***

"Are you here alone?" his deep baritone voice asked. He didn't wait for an answer but began to pull out the chair across from her and sat down. The smug look on his face dared her to try and send him away. Little did he know Sidney didn't back down to dares very easily.

"Yes and I'd like to keep it that way." The lie rolled easily off her tongue. Sure she wanted him here, but she'd never say that to him. His eyes told her he already thought highly of himself. Not that he wasn't worthy. He was very worthy, but walking god or not, no way would she let him walk all over her.

"You sure about that, Sugar? I think it would be much more fun if I joined you."

Oh yeah. He was right about that.

Sidney's reading started running though her mind. The Emperor card, meeting someone new, doing something out of the ordinary, having a little fun, isn't that what Abby said? Hell, she could handle having a little bit of fun. Who was she to argue with the cards?

"One drink," Sidney said to him before sipping the last of the water in her glass.

"We'll see," was his only reply as he cocked his head in the direction of the waitress. She didn't need to be asked twice. The brunette raced over to their table obviously eager to wait on him. "Scotch, on the rocks." He ordered before both the waitress and her mystery man looked over at Sidney waiting for her to order as well.

"I'll just take another ice water." All she needed was alcohol tonight. She felt her body awakening to this man in just the ninety seconds since she'd seen him. An ache formed in her belly and traveled slightly south. Her body craved him. No doubt a couple drinks would send her right over the edge to doing something she'd regret.

Mr. Blue eyes leaned in toward her. As his eyes caressed her body, goose bumps pebbled on her skin.

"Are you sure you don't want anything with more of a kick, Sugar?"

Shaking herself free from the trance he had her in, Sidney turned towards the waitress. "An ice water." Sidney leaned backwards in her chair to bring more space between them. She winked to her table mate before turning to the waitress again, "with a lemon wedge on the side."

The waitress stalked away with heavy steps. She obviously thought she was crazy for not engaging in a little bit of alcoholic drink with the man sitting across from her. Just one look from him told her she didn't need anything to drink to fold to this man. She couldn't let that happen.

A smooth, sexy laugh snapped her attention back toward the man sitting across from her. "Lemon wasn't quite the kind of kick I was talking about but now I'm thinking you might have been on the right track anyway. If you have anything with alcohol my plans for tonight would be shot to hell. I don't take advantage of a woman who has been drinking."

Oh man this guy is cocky. "What makes you think I'm interested in whatever you have planned?"

He returned the wink she'd sent him minutes before. "You're interested, Sugar. You're just too strong-willed to admit it."

Yep, she was definitely interested. She felt her breasts tingle. Her body betrayed her. Sid never had a one night stand in her life. Well, not on purpose at least. Right now her body begged her to do it, to give into what she knew she couldn't do. That didn't sit well.

"So sure of yourself are you?"

"Yes."

Okay. He definitely didn't lack any self-confidence. Cocky men so weren't her thing but he had her body blazing with desire anyway.

She opened her lips to send him away, but her mouth had a mind of its own. "What's your name?" *Damn it. Why did I ask that?*

He cocked his brows smugly before replying, "Questions from the woman who isn't interested?"

"I was just making conversation since its obvious you don't plan on leaving my table any time soon."

He obviously decided to play along by answering her question. One look told her he knew she was lying just as much as she did. "Trenton Stone. Do I get to ask questions too?"

"Sure," Sidney replied hoping the loud beat of her heart couldn't be heard across the table.

"Okay. Tit for tat. What's your name?"

"Sidney," she blurted out. "Sidney Clark."

"What do you do for a living, Sidney?"

Oh God. The way her name rolled off his tongue made her come close to a swoon. Sidney didn't swoon.

"I own a shop called, Mystic Boutique with my best friend, Abby. I sell books, crystals, Tarot cards, that kind of thing, and Abby does readings." Depending on his reply Sid would either ditch their conversation right now and head up to her room, or she'd play his game for a little bit longer, see where it might take them.

Most people gave her a look like she was crazy when she told them about Mystic Boutique. People always scoffed at what they didn't understand. As long as they didn't look down on her for it, Sid didn't care if it was their thing or not. Not everyone was into it, but she didn't like to be judged for her shop either.

"I have to admit I don't know a lot about that kind of thing, but I think it's respectable that you're out there doing something you love."

Most men laughed at the idea of Mystic Boutique. Or they wanted to pretend she didn't do what she did. If it was possible he became even more attractive than he already was. Fear pooled in her stomach. She didn't want to like him but she did. "How do you know I love what I do?

"It's in your voice, the way it fluctuates when you mentioned your shop. That and the gleam in your eye."

Wow, she hadn't expected that answer. "Are you a psychologist or something?"

"Nope," he answered simply.

"Okay then, tit for tat, Trenton."

"I'm a graphic designer." He didn't go into anymore details with her before asking, "What are you in town for?"

Another test. Sid couldn't wait to see how he replied to this one. "Psychic fair."

Trenton didn't flinch. "I bet that's great business for you and your friend."

Sid didn't know how to reply. She'd never met someone like Trenton before and he overwhelmed her. Suit and tie kind of men usually didn't respect the kind of shop she owned. He seemed so different than anyone she'd ever known. "What are you in town for?"

"You." Trenton leaned forward, his lips capturing hers. She melted on the spot, his tongue pushing past her lips demanding entrance. Her body complied automatically letting him in. He tasted like the scotch he'd drank. She couldn't remember the waitress bringing them their drinks, but she obviously had.

His masculine, spicy scent enveloped her making a sigh emerge from the back of her throat. God she wanted this man. It was as if he'd cast a spell on her.

"Come to my room with me?" Trenton asked against her lips.

The word yes tried to break free from her lips. Just as she was about to reply she heard Abby's laughter coming from somewhere in the distance. Sid pulled away sharply. She couldn't do it. She couldn't spend one anonymous night with this man. Sex meant more to her than that. She'd promised herself a long time ago next time she was with a man it would be someone she knew she'd have a future with.

Jumping up, Sidney ran for the door.

Chapter Two

Sidney rolled over in her hotel bed. The mattress was one of the most comfortable she'd ever slept on, but it hadn't help her get any sleep last night. Trenton's sexy voice echoed through her head all night making her body primed for the pleasure she knew he'd be able to give her. She ached in places she'd almost forgotten existed. How long had it been since she'd been with a man? When you can't remember, it's been too damn long. That's what Abby would say if she asked her.

The thing was, she usually didn't give it a second thought. She had her friends, her job, and her family. That's all that really mattered. Most of the men she knew either jumped from woman to woman or she'd known them her whole life and just couldn't see them as anything more than a friend. The one time she'd thought she really found someone he proved her wrong and broke her heart.

Since then she hadn't found anyone who made her want to recant what Abby called her vow of celibacy. Until now. Her achy body pulsed just thinking about him.

Sidney sat up rising from the bed slowly. Yesterday had been the last day of the fair and she wanted to get up and checkout early. The later she stayed the bigger chance that she might run into Trenton again. He didn't strike her as the type to give up easily. With the way she'd run out on him last night, he'd want answers. She could feel it. The man had probably never been turned down by a woman in his life.

"Abbs. Wake up," Sidney said, walking over to her friend's bed to rouse her.

A groan escaped Abby's lips as she rolled over in the bed, one eye cracked open to look at Sidney. "Too early."

Sidney poked her in the side. "Get up sleepy head. We need to get out of here early. I have a few things I need to take care of back home." First thing on her list was clearing Trenton Stone out of her mind. *Yeah. Right.*

Abby got out of the bed slowly walking over to her suitcase. She grabbed her bag before heading into the bathroom. "You met him, didn't you?" she asked, standing in the doorway. "You met him and now we're escaping so you don't risk running into him again. What happened?"

Damn her. Sometimes Sid hated the fact that Abby was psychic. At times she could read her like an open book. Right now, she wasn't in the mood. She already knew how the conversation would go. She'd tell Abby about meeting the most gorgeous, sexiest man she'd ever seen. How he'd asked her up to his room, for what would no doubt be a night of hot sex, and how she'd taken off running like a scared child.

Abby would tell her how she needed to lighten up. That as long as she was safe it wouldn't hurt to have a little fun from time to time. She'd even throw in the fact that the cards read that she'd meet him and that you should never argue fate.

No, she wasn't in the mood to fight with her about it. What would be the point? Sid wasn't looking for a quick roll in the Marriot's posh sheets. Especially, with a man who captured her so intensely from the start. "I have no idea what you're talking about. Now hurry up with your shower. I still need to jump in before we head out."

***

Trenton pulled on his blue jeans before throwing a white polo shirt over his head. His eyes, heavy, rubbed like sandpaper each time he opened or closed his lids. *Damn feisty woman.* Sidney Clark hadn't left his mind since their brief run in the night before. Every time he closed his eyes he pictured her sexy blond curls bouncing around as she spoke, or the light dust of freckles that danced across the bridge of her nose.

She had the sexiest, sea green eyes he'd ever seen and a body to die for. Curvy in all the right places. At least from what he could tell as she sprinted away in the ankle length skirt she'd been wearing. Usually the woman who attracted him wore skimpy skirts and tight shirts. With Sidney, he only caught a glimpse of her behind as she ran away from him. But it had wiggled just the way he liked.

Damn, he wanted to see how it looked without that damn skirt. Even better he wanted to see her legs, he'd imagined what they would look like wrapped around his waist all night long.

And damn she could kiss. He'd only had a brief taste of her, but he already felt addicted. He craved more. Running a hand through his hair, Trenton stalked into the bathroom to throw some cold water on his face.

Something had him off his game. He never let himself dwell on a woman like he was now. He'd also never been so blatantly shut down by one either. That had to be what got to him about her. He knew women and Sidney wanted him just as much as he wanted her. The sexual tension between them sat like a heavy fog in the air. She felt it too. He knew it.

So why did she sprint away from him the way she had? Why'd she shut him down? He never got denied from a woman but she sure as hell did exactly that.

After splashing one more handful of water on his face, Trenton grabbed the standard white hotel towel and dried his face before heading back into the main room. Picking up all his belongings he started to pack his suitcase. Today was his last day in town. In a couple hours he'd be on a plane back home to Los Angeles and he'd forget about his sexy little spitfire.

The thought didn't sit right with him. Hell, he didn't know why he wanted her so bad, but he did, and Trenton was used to getting what he wanted. More than just that, she intrigued him. He found himself wanting to know more about her. He couldn't put a finger on what it was about her in particular but he planned to find out. Now. Stalking to the phone he dialed zero for the hotel desk.

"Sidney Clark's room," he said gruffly into the phone before the clerk even had a chance to spit out the whole, "thank you for calling" spiel.

"I'm sorry but that guest has already checked out," the clerk replied to him.

Shit. So she'd already taken off. Little did she know that Trenton Stone didn't give up when he wanted something, or someone. Hanging up the hotel phone without another word he pulled his sleek, black cell phone out of his pocket. It couldn't be that hard to find The Mystic Boutique.

***

Sidney lit a vanilla incense then turned to place it on the counter behind her register. About five feet away Abby sat in her reading room with the door cracked pouting because Sid still didn't want to talk to her about Trenton. Not that there was much to tell. She'd made sure of that when she ran away from him.

Walking around the counter she started rearranging a candle display. The scents of fruit mixed with her and Abby's homemade relaxation creations making her crave a snack and a nap. The couple days since they'd been back from the fair were slow around Mystic Boutique. Not scary slow but slow enough that it wasn't providing her enough to keep her mind occupied from her thoughts about Trenton and what she'd missed.

In her twenty eight years she'd never thought about sex as much as she did in the past three days. She never craved it like she did since she met the cocky, gorgeous man that wouldn't leave her dreams.

A bell jingled in the distance jerking Sid out of her daydream. "Hi. Welcome to Mys-" the words died on her tongue. Standing in her doorway stood Trenton looking sexy as sin in a pair of loose fitting jeans and a blue button up shirt. His sleeves were again rolled up to his elbows showing off his muscular forearms.

This couldn't be a coincidence. He had to be here looking for her and while the thought sent explosions of excitement shooting through her body it also put her on edge. What could he want from her? Why travel all the way to River City to see an eccentric, small town girl like herself?

Only one way to find out.

Sid took a deep breath gathering her wits before she took small steps down the plank towards Trenton.

"Hello, Sidney," Trenton's voice came out smooth as honey. He stood there looking Mr. Cool, Calm, and Collected while she felt like she wanted to trample him over while making another running escape out the door. Why did he affect her like this? Men never made her feel like she'd downed three shots of caffeine the way he did. He made her jittery in a way she wasn't used to.

"Hi. Long time no see." *Well that sounded real intelligent. It's only been a couple days since I saw him last.*

"What did you expect with the way you sprinted away from me the other night? I had a name and place of employment to go off, but I still had to make arrangements to get here."

He spoke a little too loudly for comfort. Abby was the only person here, but she'd rather her friend stayed in her reading room until she could get Trenton out of here. "Sh, someone will hear you."

"Yeah, with all the people in your store right now I guess I better keep my voice down."

"My friend Abby is here."

"And she doesn't allow men in your store or what?"

What a jerk! "No, she allows men in here. Just not the cocky ones."

Trenton leaned toward her, his masculinity invading her space in the most welcomed way. "Now that's a shame, Sugar, because I'm very *cocky*. I would have liked to show you the other night before you ran out on me. Of course, I'd be willing to give it another try. I promise you'll like what you see." He pulled away and gave her a sexy wink that turned her legs to Jell-O.

Oh yeah, she wanted to see alright.

"What do you say, Sidney? I didn't get to see nearly enough of you the other night. But what I did see intrigued me. I haven't been able to get you out of my mind since Sunday night."

Sidney could tell he was just trying to get a rise out of her. It almost worked but she made herself find her tongue. He wouldn't turn her into a giggling school girl. "You weren't as memorable. I'd almost completely forgotten we'd met until you walked into my store." It was a bold faced lie, but the look on his face made it worth it. She doubted anyone would find Trenton Stone forgettable. She sure didn't, but it would be a cold day in hell before she let him know it.

The fact was, she wanted him and he knew it. What she couldn't figure out is why he wanted her so much? Why did he come all the way here to find her? Not knowing made her want him more. That scared her. She never reacted to a man this way. It wasn't smart to start now. Especially with one who lived God only knew where. It's not like they could have more than a night together.

In the blink of an eye the shocked expression on his face turned into one of amusement. The left side of his mouth raised in a crooked smile that almost had her jumping him right there. This man had way too much control over her body for someone she didn't even know.

"I haven't given you anything to remember yet, Sugar. Once I have, I promise you, you'll never forget it." His voice wrapped around her, tickling her bare arms, leaving goose bumps in its wake.

The space between them became less and less as Sid felt herself moving towards him. She couldn't have stopped if she tried. She wanted him to make good on his promise. It wasn't smart, but in this moment she didn't care.

"Um, am I interrupting something?" Sid spun around to see Abby peaking her head out of the door watching them. Shit, how did she forget Abby was here? She'd never hear the end of this one. And damned if she didn't feel a wave of disappointment wash over her that Abby interrupted what she knew would have been one hot kiss.

Stepping back out of arms reach from Trenton, Sidney focused her attention on Abby. "Of course you aren't."

Abby smiled a knowing smile. "Are you sure? I planned to come out and stretch my legs, but if you need any privacy I could-"

"No."

"Yes," Trenton added at the same time.

Sid heard him groan as Abby walked out the door. Sidney came forward meeting her friend halfway at the register. Even though she'd been the one who had initiated their almost kiss she was glad for the distraction. One kiss would no doubt lead to another and even though she craved this man, she knew she couldn't let herself get that close to him.

"Abby, this is Trenton Stone. We met briefly in Portland and now he's passing through and stopped to say hi." Turning to Trenton as he stepped up beside her, Sid continued, "Trenton this is my best friend and business partner, Abby Gold."

Abby looked like she knew a little too much for comfort. Trenton reached out and grabbed her hand in a firm shake. "Nice to meet you, Abby."

"It's nice to meet you too. How long will you be in town?"

Trenton's eyes landed on Sidney when he replied. "I'm not sure yet. I came to town with a goal in mind and I don't plan on leaving until I accomplish it."

So not what she wanted to hear. "What about work? Don't you have to be back to work any time soon?" Sid asked him.

"As long as I have my lap top and my wireless, I can work from anywhere." Sidney could tell he enjoyed every minute of this. He liked watching her squirm and reach for straws on how to get him out of town.

"You'll love it here," Abby cut in. "It's a great place for a vacation. I'm sure Sid would love to show you around some time."

Sidney jabbed her in the ribs. Her *ex*-best friend would get it when Trenton left.

"I'm counting on Sidney showing me a lot of things while I'm in town." Trenton again directed his reply to Abby at Sidney.

Perfect timing, the phone rang giving Sid the chance to escape Abby and Trenton who she felt were beginning to gang up on her. "I'm expecting a call. I'll be right back," she said before bolting toward her office where she'd left the cordless earlier. Behind her she closed the door with a bang.

***

Trenton watched Abby eye him, a smirk on her rounded face. He could tell she had something on her mind so he waited for her to go ahead and spit it out. He knew it had something to do with Sidney. Maybe it would give him a little more insight into her. All he knew so far is what she did for a living and she liked to drive him crazy.

In a good way.

She gave him a hard time like no woman he'd ever known and that was refreshing for some reason. Any other woman would be bending to his every wish by now. Even though he liked it that way, something about the way she made him work for it felt good too. Still he did intend to get his way with her.

"You like her," Abby finally said to him. He immediately noticed the fact that her words were made as a statement not a question.

"I don't know her."

"It doesn't matter. You still like her."

He thought about denying her claim, but he didn't. Trenton didn't shy down to who or what he was even if he didn't understand it right now. He would never be ashamed of the man he was.

"I like what I know about her. I want her. That's about the end of it." Which was true. He did like her, but this wasn't about anything more than getting what he wanted. More than anything, he wanted a night with Sidney Clark. Maybe two. He'd do whatever it took to have her.

Abby smiled at him like she knew some deep, dark secret that he didn't know. "Listen," he told her. "I don't want you to read anything more into this than what it is. I'm being truthful with Sidney and I don't want her to get the feeling from you that she can expect more than what I want to give her."

Abby's smile didn't falter as she watched him in what looked like amusement. He wasn't amused and didn't like to be the source of her amusement. Time to get out of here. "Can you just tell Sidney I'll be back a little later to finish our conversation?"

"No," Abby told him. "Don't go running off. I didn't mean to insult your manhood or anything."

"It's impossible to insult me, Sweetheart. I have no doubts about my manhood."

Abby gave him a chuckle. "I didn't expect you to be this cocksure."

He didn't know what she meant by that. Had Sidney told her about him? She acted as if she knew something about him or expected to meet him. "This is me. I won't change for anyone."

"I'm not asking you to change, but I do have some advice for you."

Just fucking great.

"I'll be quick about this. I know you want Sid, but you're going about it all wrong. If you want her, you'll have to get to know her first. She isn't the type that's going to just jump into bed with someone she doesn't know."

"If she's looking for a proposal or something, she won't find it here."

"I'm not saying you have to marry her. All I'm saying is if you want her as much as you say you do, you're going to have to work a little bit harder to get her."

Abby turned and headed back into the room she'd come from closing the door behind her. Sidney was still closed away in another room as well. Pacing the small store he thought about what Abby said to him. He never went through this much trouble for a woman. He went out from time to time with women, but on his terms. When and where he wanted.

Trenton didn't like being told that he had to do something which is pretty much what Abby said to him. Did he really want her bad enough to go through all the wining and dining? She wasn't his type at all. They'd never be able to have any kind of relationship past a couple days.

But he had come all the way to River City or whatever the hell the little hole in the wall town she lived in was called.

Wasn't that enough?

Trenton turned as he heard the door open. Sidney came out a smile on her face, her cute little freckles catching his eye. It wasn't enough. He knew at that moment he would do whatever it took to have this woman. His desire for her was too strong not to do whatever it took.

"Have dinner with me tonight." Sidney looked shocked. Before she had the chance to turn him down he added, "Just dinner. I promise. Nothing more."

She looked at him with a twinkle in her eye that made him want to promise her the world. Since when did he turn into such a sap? It pissed him off but he couldn't do anything to change the way he felt.

"Sure. I'll have dinner with you," she finally replied.

His body soared and his cock hardened at the thought of spending more time with her. *Down boy. It's just a dinner.*

"I'll pick you up here at seven." Trenton turned and stalked towards the door, "And wear something sexy."

Chapter Three

Why did I agree to do this? Sidney wandered around The Mystic Boutique, nervous energy moving her hands to straighten the same rack of dresses for the third time. What was the point of the whole dinner? All he wants is a quick roll in the hay and she didn't do that. Not since Ivan. But then with Ivan she hadn't known that's all it would be. She thought she actually meant something to him.

What a joke.

Now here she was going out with a man who she knew only wanted the same thing Ivan had. *Stupid, stupid, stupid.* That's what pissed her off the most. She wasn't a stupid woman but apparently where men were concerned she lost every shred of knowledge she had.

Glancing up at the moon and stars clock behind the counter to see Trenton would be here any minute. Sid grazed her hands down her white tank top and dark blue peasant skirt. It wasn't much of an outfit but the way she saw it, it wasn't much of a date either. All she'd done was play into his attempt to get in her pants. Or under her skirt as the situation saw fit.

She sure as hell didn't plan to try and impress him. She was a tank top kind of girl and that wouldn't change for Mr. Big City who found himself in her comfortable, one horse town. Even if he was drop dead gorgeous.

The air filled with the sound of a rasping on the glass door. Show time. Sid walked over and unlocked the door. She usually never locked it when she was there after hours. Everyone knew the Boutique closed at five so they didn't bother her if she was there late. Life was like that in her small town. Today she'd made sure to lock up. She didn't want to take the chance that Trenton could sneak up on her.

She opened the door to Trenton wearing the same pair of jeans but this time he donned a black Oxford shirt. Although he didn't dress up as much as some of the business types she'd seen before, he stood out like a sore thumb in River City. But then it probably wasn't the clothes that did that. He held an air of strength and superiority about him. From what Sid could tell he wasn't the type to think himself better than anyone else, he just exuded a self confidence she'd never witnessed before.

His eyes pierced her while she stood there watching him. Her stomach did flip flops making her a bit nauseated. Pushing her doubts aside Sid gave him a small wave. "Hi. Nice to see you again." Nice put it lightly. *I'm in so much trouble.* Just twenty seconds in his presence and her body was already on fire for him.

Trenton didn't answer but bent and captured her lips with his. Sid felt her body immediately melt into his as she opened her mouth to give him access. His tongue skillfully dove into her mouth igniting bursts of pleasure to explode throughout her body. As his strong arms enclosed her, his heat radiated off him resulting in her own body temperature rising.

He wanted her as much as she wanted him. Her defenses weakened the longer his mouth mated with hers. Seconds later she felt his large hands smooth down her back as they began to cup her behind. *Not again!*

She pulled away sharply. "I agreed to go out to dinner with you, Trenton. That's all. If you have more in mind than that we can just call it a night right now."

He pulled away as well, his molten stare making her want to erase her statement. She doubted any woman had ever shot him down like she was. Hell, if things were different, she'd be jumping in the sack with him as well. But the reality was things weren't different. He wanted one thing from her and she wasn't going to give it away as freely as she did with Ivan.

No man would take advantage of her like that again.

The longer they stood there the more she thought he'd turn and walk away. Why would he wait around for her when he could have any woman he wanted? Seconds before she planned to turn and walk back into her boutique Trenton's smooth, strong hand grabbed hers.

"You're going to be the death of me, woman," he said with a smile and a wink. His confidence not even dented from her denial. "Let's get out of here."

Following him out the door, Sid grabbed her keys from her small black purse and locked up. "Where are we going?"

"I saw a little restaurant across the street from my hotel room. I figured we go there. I think they have tables out by the river."

Sidney almost laughed. She'd grown up eating at Riverside Restaurant and Lounge. Being so used to the big city, Trenton spoke to her about the place like he was telling her about it for the first time. There were so many different restaurants where he came from he probably never brought a date to the same place twice. She didn't want to embarrass him by bringing it up though. Not that anything would embarrass Trenton Stone.

"It looks like a nice place to eat," he continued as they walked down Main Street.

"I think you just like the close proximity to your hotel room. Are you going to try and take advantage of me again tonight?" she kidded. She enjoyed the easy banter between them. They'd started off with it in Portland and it carried over to his surprise trip here. When they joked around it made her feel more at ease with him. More like they knew each other rather than the strangers they were.

When Trenton reached out and grabbed her hand again a tingle formed in her fingers, shooting up her arm. Damn he had an effect on her body. "Will you let me?"

Yes. "No."

"Now why did I know you'd say that?"

"Because you're starting to learn that you can't always get what you want?" Yeah, right. She knew if he wanted it bad enough, a man like him could always get what he wanted. She was inches away from giving into him herself.

He had the gall to laugh at her words. Apparently he knew just as well as she did his effect on people. "I always get what I want, Sugar. Sooner or later." Stopping in front of a black Mustang convertible Trenton clicked a button on his key ring to unlock the door before opening it.

"Ladies first."

Inhaling a deep breath as a slight wind tickled across her skin Sidney shut the door Trenton held open for her. The air blew fresh and crisp. Fall was just around the corner which meant rain was on the way. This was the perfect time a year, still warm and sunny afternoons, but the evening cooled to contrast the days.

"It's a beautiful night. Riverside's only about three blocks up the road. Do you mind if we walk?" Sidney asked. He looked shocked by her words, but agreed.

"Sounds good to me. Just let me grab something out of my car."

Trenton opened the back door grabbing what looked like a light jacket before he closed the door behind him and joined her again. "Ready?"

"Yep." As they started to walk Sidney was again surprised when he reached out to grab her hand.

***

He couldn't stop himself from touching her in anyway possible. The only time she didn't pull away is when he held her hand so that's what he did. God, when was the last time he'd walked hand and hand with a woman? He couldn't remember. It seemed too intimate which didn't make sense at all since what he really wanted to do was lay her down and strip her naked. But no matter how it felt he couldn't stop himself from doing it.

Her skin was so soft. Her petite hand fit so snug in his much larger one. This whole damn situation didn't make any sense. At thirty two years old he was chasing a woman for the first time. A woman he didn't even know, a woman who didn't even live in the same state he did, but for the life of him he couldn't walk away from her.

Why? It was unsettling to admit even to himself. He didn't have the answer and that grated on his nerves. He was an answer man. He always knew what to say, do, and was always in charge. The only way to get the answers he sought was to play the game. Spend time with her and find out what about her made him so rock hard with need.

Still, he'd find a way to do it on his terms. He always got what he wanted and this wouldn't be any different. And when he did finally have Sidney, it would be the best night she'd ever had.

***

They walked into the small, dimly lit restaurant to a hostess with a fake smile on her face. The scent of spices permeated the air. As Trenton stepped closer the young woman did a double take at him, then Sidney, before her smile grew to stretch across her face. Sidney's body went ridged against his as she tried to pull her hand from his. He tightened his grip not enough to hurt, but enough so she knew he wouldn't give in.

"Hello, Sidney." The hostess's eyes twinkled as she looked between Sidney and himself. "Table for two?"

"Yes," Trenton said shortly. He didn't like the gleam in her eyes. She obviously had something up her sleeve. "I'd like a table outside." He'd already planned to enjoy the fresh air while they ate, but liked the idea even more since seeing the hostess. She made Sidney uncomfortable and he wanted this night to be as stress free as possible for her.

"I didn't know you were dating anyone, Sid. Another out of town man at that," the hostess said with a sneer.

He felt Sidney's posture straighten as she looked the woman in the eyes. "I didn't realize my dating life was any of your business, Mandy."

"Just being a caring friend. I wouldn't want you to get your heart broken like you did last time."

As the words left her mouth anger and sadness rolled off Sidney. She opened her mouth to speak, but nothing came out. Trenton had the overwhelming urge to take care of her. He didn't know what was going on between the two ladies, but he wouldn't stand here and let the woman harass his date.

"Since you don't know how to do your job, we'll seat ourselves. I'd appreciate it if you stayed away from us for the rest of the evening." Trenton reached over and grabbed two menus from the stand and started weaving his way through the tables toward the back door. Sidney followed along without putting up a fight.

"Excuse me." Trenton stopped the waitress outside. "You hostess didn't seem to want to bring us to our seats so I took it upon myself. Can you direct us to a seat?"

"Mandy has a hair up her butt again huh, Sid?" The waitress said.

Damn, he'd forgotten everyone in this town knew each other. It was so foreign to him. He only had a couple friends who he let close enough to know anything about him. He damn sure didn't know all the waitresses and hostesses in his local restaurants.

"You know how she gets. The mouth is just looking for gossip to spread around."

"I hear ya. Go ahead and have a seat you two and I'll be over to get your drink orders in a minute."

Trenton led Sidney to the small square table at the far edge of the outside dining area. The air began to cool and a slight wind blew across the river towards them. They had small heating poles placed around the dining area along with a few dim lights. The atmosphere felt much more romantic than he had planned, but comfortable all the same.

Holding her chair out for her, he placed the long sleeved shirt he'd grabbed out of the rental car around her. "Sorry it's not much, but it should keep the edge off."

Sidney looked surprised by his generosity but recovered quickly and took the seat he offered to her. "Thanks."

"Not a problem." Trenton sat in the chair across from her. She still looked upset and that bothered him. "If you don't give me a smile, Sugar, I'm going to have to give you something to smile about." And he knew he could. He knew she knew he could, but she wouldn't want to admit it to him. In some ways she was just as proud as he was. Who'd have known that would be such a turn on?

"What makes you think you could give me a reason to smile?" she asked her sassiness returning. A slight wind blew a curl in her face. Trenton itched to reach out and put it behind her ear but she did the honors before he had the chance.

"We both know I could make you smile. Make you scream, writhe, cry, burst into a million different pieces from pleasure." Her cheeks turned crimson with his words and damn if he didn't start to harden. "I can't wait for that last part, Sidney. Its going to be so much fun watching you come undone."

He watched her shift in her chair, her eyes widening with his words. She looked so sweet and innocent. From the two kisses they shared he knew better than to think Sidney Clark innocent. Inside her burned a passionate fire that he couldn't wait to ignite. "No snappy comeback Ms. Clark?" he mocked.

A look of relief crept across her face as the waitress they'd spoken to earlier stepped up to the table.

"Saved by the bell," he said the words not caring if the waitress heard.

"Excuse me?" she asked.

"Nothing," Sidney told her. "I need something with a little kick in it tonight, Sally. What drink do you suggest?"

Chapter Four

Sidney ordered a sex on the beach at Sally's suggestion. She didn't drink often so she had no idea what she was in for. Trenton's sexy words had her feeling a little bit frisky, feeling like she wanted to live on the edge. To her surprise, Trenton ordered an iced tea before Sally slipped away to get their drinks.

Damn the man knew how to get her hormones up and running. Men in River City didn't talk to her like he did. It made her feel sexy and carefree. Should she let herself feel that way? In the end she'd still be the same ole Sid. The one who wanted more out of sex than just a hot time between the sheets. A small town girl who could never hold onto a man like Trenton. Hell, she didn't even know if she wanted too. They still didn't know very much about each other.

Like he read her mind, Trenton asked, "Have you lived here long?"

Sidney laughed. "Yeah. Twenty eight years to be exact."

"Really," he looked perplexed. "How do you do it?"

"What do you mean? This is my home. I love it here." And she did. Sure there were your downfalls,

Mandy the mouth being one of them. Everyone always knew everyone else's business, secrets spread like wildfires, and there wasn't a lot to do, but it was still home.

"I don't do the whole small town thing. Seems like the same ole thing everyday. You see the same faces and places. Your business isn't your own. People look at me like I'm a two headed monster around here. Not that I care."

He just proved her point about him without even knowing it. No way could she let herself be with this man. All he wanted was to win his prize and be on his way. She wouldn't be any man's prize. Not in the way he looked for at least.

"All of that is true but you aren't looking at the positives, just the negatives. I have great friends who I have known my whole life. If someone needs help, the whole town pitches in and does what they can for each other. People smile when you walk by. The grocer knows what you want the second you step up to the counter, that kind of thing. You can't beat it."

He looked to be deep in thought for a moment. His brows creased, his eyes had a far off expression. She thought just maybe he was really thinking about what she had to say. So many people she'd met looked down at small town life. Like they were missing so much because of the lives they chose to live. For some reason she didn't want Trenton to feel that way. His opinion mattered to her.

"That might be the kind of life you enjoy, Sugar, but it isn't for me."

He said the words, but they didn't ring true to her ears. *Wishful thinking, Sid. You have the hot's for him so your looking for hope where there isn't any.* She felt a connection with him that she didn't understand. Part of it was physical, but deep in her soul she knew there was more. What, she didn't know. Her heart wanted to explore the connection, but her brain thought better of it.

"Whatever you say, Stone. Since this isn't the life for you why don't you enlighten me? What is the kind of life that is for you?"

"Exactly the kind of life I live. Working for myself, not having anyone to answer to. If I feel like going somewhere, I go. I don't want anyone to answer to. I like to go out, have a good time, meet new and interesting people, that kind of thing."

"So basically, no one close to you? No one to care about you? Nothing too serious?"

He winked at her before saying, "don't make it sound so bad, Sidney. Nothing holds me back. I like to have what I want when I want it, the way I live my life, I'm free to do that. It works for me."

"You know what I think?" Sidney asked before taking a sip of her Sex on the beach. "I think you're fooling yourself. If you think that will make you happy for the long run, you're crazy."

"Is that so? When did you get to know me so well?"

"I don't. Call it women's intuition, but I don't think you're as big and bad as you want people to think you are." She felt her words were true. Was she playing herself? Believing what she wanted so that she could give in to his wishes?

He leaned in towards her talking in a whisper. "Why don't we call the rest of this dinner off and go to my hotel room. I'll show you how bad I can be."

***

He had to let her know how it was. She fooled herself if she thought he was anything different than what he was, a man looking to have a good time. With her. That's all. There would be no grand declarations of love, nor promises of a future. He couldn't imagine living with one woman for the rest of his life. And while he enjoyed the relaxed pace of River City, it wasn't anything he planned to get used to. He'd get bored, go stir crazy in a place like this.

"I can be very bad, Sidney. I like it that way and you'll like it too. I can promise you that and nothing else." The look in her eyes made him want to stop talking. She looked disappointed and for the first time in his life he cared what someone else thought about him, but if he stopped, if he didn't let her know how it was, he ran the risk of hurting her.

Sure they didn't know each other well enough for feelings to be involved right now, but he couldn't risk it. He liked to play the field, but leaving a trail of broken hearted women wasn't his thing. They all knew the score up front.

"I want you, I plan to have you, but that's all. I can offer you nothing but a night or two of extreme pleasure. There are no hidden meanings or feelings behind anything I say. I'm a straight shooter."

God the words sounded harsh even to his own ears, but they were true. He kept his eyes locked on Sidney's as she took in what he said. She took another couple drinks before she finally spoke.

"I wasn't asking for grand declarations as you put it, Stone. Just making an observation." She took her last drink before setting her glass back on the table. "Plus, I won't be sleeping with you anyway so you just wasted a good speech for nothing."

"You guys looked deep in conversation so I gave you a little bit of extra time," Sally the waitress said as she walked up to their table. "Are you ready to order yet or do you need more time?"

Trenton eyed Sidney as she calmly ordered the special of the night. He quietly thanked God when she ordered an ice tea as well instead of another drink. He wanted her to have a clear head tonight. If she'd had another drink any possibility of spending the night with her would be shot.

Taking a quick glance at the menu he ordered the biggest steak they had before handing the menu to their waitress. Sitting there he watched Sidney in silence. He had a lot of respect for her. More than anyone he'd met in a long time if not ever. She knew who she was, what she wanted. She didn't shake easily and when he did stir her up she calmed herself quickly.

Although he didn't understand her love of the small town she lived in, he respected it all the same. She knew where she belonged and defended it with all she had. Everything he learned about her made him want her more. She riled him like no other woman he'd ever met.

"So, where are you from, Trenton? I've been meaning to ask you that."

"Los Angeles," he answered simply.

"I knew you were a big city boy. Born and raised?"

"No. I made my escape there when I was eighteen. I put myself through college, started my career and never looked back." Almost never.

"Where'd you escape from?"

"A little town in Georgia. About the size of River City actually," he could think of a lot of things he'd rather talk about than his past. The red head in Sidney's store said she'd want to get to know him better so that's what he'd do. Really he wanted to get to know her. Inside and out although that didn't sit too comfortably with him. But he was a fighter, strong and proud. A little bit of discomfort wouldn't send him running.

Something sparked in her eyes before she spoke again. It lit up her green depths and made him want to bask in that light. *What the fuck am I thinking? Bask in her light. I sound like a damn woman.*

"Well I never would have thought. Trenton Stone is a small town boy at heart. I wondered where the Sugar kept coming from." She took a drink of her ice tea. Sally the waitress was good. He hadn't seen her slip the drink on their table. As she set her glass down a bead of condensation dripped down her finger. He watched in awe as Sidney licked the droplet of water off her hand. His cock stirred. She didn't realize how sexy he found her.

Damn he needed to get some. It had been a few months. He didn't realize he itched so badly for female companionship until he ran into the curly haired, sweetheart. *It's not any female companionship you're wanting. It's her. There's something different about her.*

Trenton pushed his insane thoughts aside. He didn't even know her. Even if he did he wasn't the type to settle down with a woman. Especially one who would want to tie him down in small town USA. "The words small and boy have no room in a sentence about me."

All of a sudden a burst of laughter erupted from deep within Sidney's body. Her breasts shook with her heavy laughter. The sounds were musical, beautiful. Had he ever heard anything as magical as Sidney's joy? It almost made him forget the fact that she was laughing at him. Almost.

"Something funny?" he asked. His voice came out irritated, but he didn't care.

A few seconds later she calmed herself enough to speak. "You," she replied.

Hmm. Trenton didn't get called funny too often. He wasn't sure he liked it. "You plan to enlighten me on the joke?"

"The words small and boy have no room in a sentence about me," she mocked. "You never give up do you?"

Part of him wanted to laugh himself. The line did sound a bit cheesy when she repeated it. But it was true. He knew it and she knew it too. Scooting his chair closer to hers Trenton grabbed her hand under the table and set it on the hard, long erection trying to burst free from his pants. He could see the shock in her eyes with is bold move, but she didn't pull away.

"I've never given up on anything in my life, Sidney. I don't plan to start now. Even if I wanted to, this would stop me." He ground her hand against his shaft to prove his point, but also driving himself crazy in the process. For a minute she held herself still, letting him work himself with her petite hand. The table cloth covered their actions from anyone at nearby tables. She felt so good he wanted to lose it right there.

She ground her hand against him this time of her own accord. He'd never wanted anyone as bad as he did at this moment. A low, steady growl escaped his lips.

"Dinner is served." Sally set a plate down in front of each of them oblivious to what she'd interrupted. Sidney yanked her hand away obviously just as startled by the other woman's arrival as he was. Maybe she wasn't such a good waitress after all.

***

Sid couldn't believe what just happened. If Sally hadn't come along it would have continued to happen too. His heat scorched her through his pants. And he was right, there was nothing small about Trenton Stone. He was all man beneath those blue jeans and she yearned to have him even more.

Picking her mind for some kind of conversation starter she remembered his words about escaping his small town. She'd seen something different in his eyes. He had wanted to escape something more than just the town she'd put money on it. *What is with me? I'm not Abby. She's the psychic one I'm just a dreamer.* Still the thought wouldn't shake from her mind. *Should I ask him?* She wanted to, but something told her that was a rough spot with Trenton. After what just happened beneath the table she wanted something light to talk about. Something they'd both enjoy and something that had nothing to do with sex.

Trenton moved his chair back over to the other side of the table taking his plate along with him. He watched her while he made his movements. His eyes entranced her, captured her. Her breasts began to feel heavy, the apex of her thighs ached.

"You better stop looking at me like that, Sidney, or you're going to be in a whole lot of trouble." Calm as can be he cut into his steak and took a bite.

Chapter Five

Sexual tension clouded the air around them. He could still feel her small hand on his cock. He'd pulsed and flexed beneath her wanting to break free from his confining jeans. If they hadn't been at the damn restaurant he knew they'd be in bed right now. The look of delight and need on her face when she touched him was too strong to ignore. He felt it. She felt it. The evidence blossomed in her bright green eyes.

Damn, if her hand felt that good he couldn't wait to feel her silky heat wrapped around him. He had to have her. He would have her. Nothing would get in his way, not now. For the first time he felt obsessed with someone. Was it because she kept turning him down? It had to be. *She's just a woman. No different than any of the others I've had in the past.* The words didn't ring true but damned if he wanted to think about that right now.

Cutting into his steak, Trenton took another bite before raising his eyes to Sidney. As soon as he made eye contact her orbs sharply diverted downward towards the food she'd hardly touched. Her hand absently pushed her fork in circles mixing the food on her plate. "Thinking about skipping the meal and heading straight home for dessert? Sounds like a hell of a plan to me." He knew he goaded her, but couldn't help himself. Trenton found himself on edge waiting to hear her next witty reply.

"No thanks," she replied. "I'm not much of a dessert person. It's usually a disappointment. I find it always looks much better than it actually is."

Trenton laughed. He couldn't help himself. She kept him on his toes and that felt damn good. Much different than what he was used to. "Sugar, if you think the package is good, you should taste what's inside. Nobody can eat just one."

"Well I guess its good I don't plan on having a taste."

Now she didn't seem so amusing. Why was she fighting their attraction so strongly? It bothered him that she seemed to have something against him. He wasn't so bad a guy. He spelled out to her up front what the score would be. Not all men would do that. It was hard for him to understand people who didn't just go for what they wanted. He'd never known any different.

***

Sidney and Trenton finished their dinner making small talk. They ate and chatted about their lives getting to know more about each other. He learned so much about her life in River City. Coming from her mouth it sounded almost pleasant, like some kind of dream or old TV show where everyone one was happy and friendly. He half expected The Beav to go traipsing through the restaurant at any moment.

You had that once? Was it really as bad as you remember?

He watched her talk animatedly about her friend and her life only pausing to breathe. He couldn't turn away from her for the life of him. *This is happiness. She is truly happy with her life.* But then he was happy too. Maybe not as happy as she was, but that wasn't his style anyway. He didn't do giddy happy. She almost made him want to.

It's your dick, man. He knew it wasn't the head on top of his neck doing the thinking where Sidney Clark was concerned. It couldn't be. He'd be in trouble if it was because he was thinking all sorts of crazy thoughts sitting here watching her talk. Thoughts that involved more than just the two of them burning up the sheets together. Thoughts that had no business sneaking their way into his head. Thoughts that surprised him, scared him.

"From the look on your face I can tell I'm boring you to death," she said to him before taking a drink of her tea.

He could feel the worried expression on is face, but it hadn't been due to her boring him. Hell, she was the most interesting woman he'd ever known. It had to do with the way she made him feel, what she made him think. Not that he could peg what exactly she brought out in him, but he knew it was different than anything he'd experienced before. *This is about sex, Stone. Nothing more, nothing less.*

"Naw, you're not boring me. I was just trying to see the town through your eyes. I don't see what you do when I look around."

"That's because you're not really looking. You don't want to see it." A light wind brushed across them making Sidney bury herself in Trenton's shirt.

"It's getting cold, Sugar. We better get going." He signaled the waitress over who brought their check. After paying for the meal, Trenton helped Sidney from her chair and they made their way around front to the road.

"I have a nice, comfortable room right across the street. What do you say," he raised his hand and began drawing circles on her soft cheek with the pad of this thumb. His body burned with need. She felt so soft, so sweet that he couldn't stop himself from leaning forward and placing a light kiss on her pouty lips.

He didn't rush her, didn't push his way inside, just placed gentle kisses one after another enjoying the feel of her mouth against his. As she always did she responded her body molded against his as their lips found a rhythm. She tasted sweet and sugary. A slight strawberry scent tickled his nose.

"You smell sweet and taste even better," he said against her lips. "I want to devour you, Sidney. Are you going to let me?" If she didn't he'd fucking explode. He struggled to contain himself just waiting for her to answer. "What do you say, Sid? Come to my room with me."

***

Hearing her nickname whispered from his lips almost did her in. Everyone called her Sid. She'd grown up with the name so why did it sound so much different coming from Trenton? Why did if feel like that name was meant to be uttered from his lips for only her? It made her want to say yes. *He* made her want to say yes, but she couldn't do it.

If there'd been the slightest bit of doubt before it disappeared with the nickname, with the kisses. She knew now that if they did ever make love it would be anything but casual sex. For her at least. Not for Trenton. He made that perfectly clear to her. No matter how much she wanted to say yes she couldn't. Why open herself up to be hurt like that?

Peeling herself apart from Trenton's strong, warm body, Sidney looked up and into his eyes. "I can't. I'm sorry." *Why can't I? Why can't I be strong enough to give into what my body wants and then be able to say goodbye afterward?*

He looked pained, but let her pull away. "Don't be sorry, Sugar. Come on, let's get you back to your car."

Part of her stood there in shock because of Trenton's words, but the other part of her wasn't surprised. No matter what, she knew he was a good guy. He may flirt endlessly, but he would never pressure her into something unless he knew it's what she wanted.

They turned and started their walk back to Mystic Boutique where her car waited. This time Trenton didn't reach out to grab her hand. Foolishly she missed his touch. *Stupid, stupid, stupid.* What was it about this guy? She couldn't put her finger on it and she feared that she'd never have the chance to find out. This would probably be the last time she saw him. Why would a man like him waste his time here, waiting on her when he could go back to Los Angeles and have any woman he wanted?

Though they walked slowly the trip back to her car seemed to happen in three seconds flat. With each step they took she knew she was closer and closer to saying goodbye to Trenton Stone. *That's what you want, remember? Say goodbye now before you really get hurt.*

"Here's my car," Sidney told him as they came to a stop in front of her Toyota Corolla.

Trenton led her to the driver side. "So what else is there to do around this town?"

Sid thought for a moment a little taken back by his question. "Well, it depends on what you like to do. Rafting down the river is a big one for us. There's probably only a couple weeks left before it will be too cold to go."

"Perfect. Go rafting with me tomorrow."

Her automatic response was to tell him no, but she stopped herself. It's not like he really asked anyway. He more so ordered her to go with him. Not only that, but she knew it wasn't smart to spend more time with him. It opened her up for more hurt.

No matter how much of a mistake she knew it would be she couldn't say no. Never mind the fact that he only wanted her for sex, he was leaving very soon, and she technically should be at work tomorrow, she wanted to go, deserved to go. Her cousin Shelby helped her with Mystic Boutique when she needed it so her job wasn't a major concern. That spot was left for her heart. *Cross that bridge when I come to it.*

"I haven't been down the river for a little while. Sounds good to me." *More like great.*

Trenton took down her phone number so he could call to get directions to her house in the morning. Sidney thought it silly for him to drive down to pick her up when his hotel was closer to the river than her house, but Trenton wouldn't have it any other way. She learned quickly that this man always got what he wanted.

When she sat tucked away in her car, the engine softly rumbling, Trenton finally leaned toward her for a kiss. *I should not want this so badly.* But she did. For a second she feared he wouldn't give her the pleasure, maybe nervous about how she would react, not wanting to push her.

After placing a swift, soft kiss on her cheek he stood up, patted the top of her car, and walked away. Damn, that hadn't been quite what she expected.

***

Trenton pulled his rental Mustang into the parking lot, Sidney's strawberry scent still surrounding him. He lifted his shirt to inhale the scent she'd left on him. Sweet. Perfect. He couldn't believe it when she turned him down again. At first, it annoyed him. Why wouldn't she give in to what they both wanted? But then he looked in her eyes and saw fear. Not fear of him, that much he knew, but there was something she was afraid of. He just didn't know what it was.

The last thing he wanted to see in her sexy, green eyes was fear. Even the fear mixed with want that filled her eyes wasn't enough. When he did have her he wanted pleasure and desire to be the only emotions on her mind.

Jumping out of his car, Trenton headed towards his hotel room. He couldn't wait for tomorrow, couldn't wait to spend more time with Sidney. And when was the last time he'd been rafting? He couldn't even remember. Tomorrow would be a perfect day: Sunshine, water, and Sidney in a bikini. What more could he ask for?

***

"I don't care if Shelby comes in or not. You will not be at work tomorrow, Sid."

Sidney rotated positions on the couch, curling her pajama clad legs under herself. Foolishly she'd called Abby when her attempts at settling down for the night failed. Thoughts of Trenton and their coming date wouldn't clear from her mind. More than ever she was confused, doubting her decision to accompany him rafting, but also knowing that no matter what, she would go. She wanted to go.

"I don't know, Abbs. I really want to go. That's the part that scares me. I shouldn't want to go this badly."

Abby sat silent for a minute before replying. "Why not? What's wrong with wanting to enjoy yourself with an extremely sexy man? Hell, every woman I know would kill to be in your place."

"Yeah, who wouldn't want to fall for a man who only wants to get you into bed before he splits out of your life forever? Sounds like every woman's dream to me." She knew she sounded bitter, but did care. She was bitter. The only man to touch her, to really move her would only be a temporary fixture in her life and there wasn't a damn thing she could do about it.

"Don't be so dramatic, Sid. Take life as it comes. You never know, it just might turn out better than you think it will."

Easy for her to say. Abby didn't fear anything. Never had. She knew how to cut off her emotions when she needed too, something Sid herself never learned. Where Sidney took more things to heart, Abby lived more freely. She didn't fear letting her heart get involved because she just didn't work that way. Not that she slept around, but Abby would have no problem indulging in a quickie and then sending Trenton on his way.

"I know I need to lighten up, Abbs. That's why I'm going tomorrow. I want to have a good time with Trenton, I'm just scared about how it will turn out."

"Don't be. It will all work out in the end."

She only wished she could be so sure.

Chapter Six

Trenton flipped his cell phone closed after getting directions to Sidney's house. He threw a black t-shirt over his head before running a hand through his short black hair, still wet from the shower. Grabbing his keys off the bedside table, Trenton slipped them into his blue jean shorts pocket and headed out to pick up his date.

His date. Damn, who'd have thought? First he stalked a woman he didn't even know to her hometown insisting that she bed him, now here he was picking her up for their second date. *What the hell am I doing here?* Having sex was never this much work. He didn't like complicated women. He wanted someone who was out to have a good time and that's it.

If that's true, why can't I get Sidney out of my head?

Trenton turned his car down Oak Street watching all the little children run and play as he went. Husbands stood in their yards doing work, fixing cars, women gardened and fed cats on their porches. His neighborhood in Los Angeles wasn't anything like this. Georgia was. For the first time since he left, he missed it.

He pulled his car into the driveway of the last house on the left just as Sidney told him to. It was a small, modest home painted a cheery yellow with flowers gracing the front porch. *It fits her,* he thought as he got out of the car and headed to the house.

"Hey," Sidney said, opening the door before he had the chance to knock.

"Miss me that much, Sugar?" he asked teasing her about answering the door so soon. He only hoped she was as eager to see him as she seemed.

Sidney's cheeks blushed lightly. "No, I just don't want to give you the opportunity to invite yourself in. Otherwise I might never get you out again."

"Are you saying I'm pushy?" he leaned against her door frame.

"You? No way!" Sidney smiled making his heart skip a beat. *What the hell was that? That's never happened before?*

"I don't call it pushy, Sid. More like strong-willed, determined. I'm very determined when I want something." He leaned in towards her, "And if you haven't noticed, I want you. I want to seduce you, want you panting my name while we have hot, sweaty, grinding sex."

Once more he leaned down so his mouth was a mere inch from her ear, "I think you want me too, Sid. I can see it in your eyes, hear it in your heavy breathing, the pulse in your throat is pounding with every word I speak." Trenton grabbed a blonde curl which slipped out of the short ponytail she had at the back of her head and pushed it behind her ear. "I like your hair like this. It looks nice." He nibbled her ear before backing away. "Are you ready to go?"

Sidney stepped forward. Instead of walking out with him she swung and punched him in the arm.

Trenton laughed. "You have a nice little swing there, Sid, but that wasn't the response I hoped for."

"You deserve it! I know what you're trying to do and I want you to know it's not going to work. You may be able to woo all your big city women with that kind of talk but it doesn't work with me."

Yeah right. "Tell that to your perk, little nipples that are standing to attention. Nice swimsuit by the way." He hadn't even noticed it before. It wasn't a bikini like he hoped, but she still looked sexy as hell in the black one piece. If he had it his way, she'd lose the cute, little white shorts she wore but it was still slightly chilly out. They had all day to lose the clothes.

Taking his eyes away from her delectable body he looked her in the eyes and quickly backed away from her again. Trenton held his hands up in surrender. "Hey, don't hit me again. I was just making an observation."

"You're terribly arrogant, you know that?" she asked with a smile.

"So I've been told. You like it though. I just wish you'd admit it."

Sidney leaned in and grabbed a bag from the inside of her house before she stepped out onto the porch with him. "Do you ever give up?"

"Not until I get what I want. You might as well give in now."

She started walking down the porch stairs, stopping to turn and look at him over her shoulder.

"Okay, I admit it. I like you a little bit. But don't think that means I plan to do anything about it." Then she walked away toward his waiting car.

If he thought she was sexy before it was nothing compared to how he felt about her now. She was beautiful, strong, feisty, and she liked him. Hot Damn.

***

Sidney couldn't believe she'd just admitted to liking Trenton. Along with the admission came a surge of pride. For the first time she'd been the one to walk away and leave him speechless. He stood on the top of her stairs while she opened the passenger door of his car and got inside. He wasn't taking his eyes off her and damn if it didn't feel good.

Reaching over she beeped the horn. Finally his long, short clad legs stepped off her porch and headed towards his car. He was masculinity personified. His short, dark hair mussed on his head were such a striking contrast to his ice blue eyes. His body was so long and lean yet his tight, cut muscles constricted, showing his obvious strength.

Oh God, how was she ever going to keep turning this man down? If he stayed in town much longer she wouldn't be able to. It was inevitable and she knew it. There was something about him that grabbed a hold on her and had yet to let go. She wondered if it ever would let go.

"Fasten your seat belt, Sid," Trenton said as he got into the car. "You're in for the ride of your life."

As soon as he spoke she had a flashback to her reading with Abby. She'd said the exact same thing to her. "That's not the first time I've heard that about you." The words accidentally slipped out of her mouth as he started the car and began to drive away. She regretted them immediately.

"What do you mean by that?" he looked worried by her words.

Smooth move, Sid. How did she fix this one? Somehow she didn't think it would go over real well if she told him Abby gave her a tarot card reading that predicted they would meet. Even though he responded well to what she and Abby did for a living, he didn't seem like the New Age type to her.

"Um, Abby warned me you'd be a handful the other day after you met at the Boutique, that's all. No big deal."

"I think Abby can be more of a handful than me."

"Maybe, but she's not as dangerous as you are."

He laughed his smooth as honey laugh that set her body on fire. "I resent that. I'm not dangerous at all."

"Oh no. You're Mr. Innocent aren't you?"

"Well, I wouldn't go that far, but I'm not dangerous."

Little did he know he was very dangerous to her heart. The more she got to know him the more dangerous he became. "I think you underestimate yourself." As soon as the words left her mouth she realized how silly they sounded. Trenton's laugh confirmed her knowledge. "Okay, maybe underestimate isn't the right word to use, but you know what I mean?"

"No I don't. Why don't you explain it to me?"

Of course he wouldn't make this easy on her. Trenton didn't make anything easy on her. She had a feeling he liked it that way. "Can we leave it at that?"

"Nope."

"You're so bossy. Take a left here," she said changing the subject.

"I know where I'm going so quit trying to change the subject. Why am I dangerous?"

Shit. "Because you're you. You're gorgeous," with that Trenton smiled. "Oh stop, you know I think you're gorgeous so don't smile like you just scored points or something."

"Well can't I revel in the fact that you finally admitted it?"

"Not if you want me to finish." When he didn't reply she continued, "You're dangerous because you make me want to do things I promised myself I wouldn't do again." She couldn't believe the admission she was making but for some reason the words rolled from her mouth all the same.

"You promised yourself you'd never sleep with a man again? I have to tell ya, that's a pretty self-defeating promise to make."

"No smart guy. I didn't promise myself I'd never sleep with another man, I just…" God, how did she say this without making it look like she felt more for him than she should? "Listen, can we drop this?"

Trenton pulled his car into the parking lot at the raft rental store and shut off the engine. Sidney couldn't bring herself to look at him. She knew he would see way more than she wanted him to if he looked into her eyes.

To her surprise he said, "Yeah, we can let it go."

Thank God.

~177~

"For now."

Of course he had to throw that in there. She grabbed the handle to open the door. Trenton grabbed her arm before she could get out.

"Hey," he said touching her face and turning it towards his. "You said earlier that I can't woo you like I do other women. I just want you to know, you don't have to tell me, I know you aren't like any other woman I've ever met." He let go of her and stepped out of the car.

Rubbing her hands together Sidney tried to compose herself. Before she knew it her right hand rose to her mouth and she chewed her nail nervously. *Don't read too much into what he said.* Damn it was hard. She wanted to be different to Trenton. The more time she spent with him the more she realized he was different to her. More so than she wanted him to be.

What did he mean? Good different or bad different? She couldn't help but think it must be good otherwise he wouldn't have brought it up in the first place. But then was that just her wishful thinking or what he'd really meant? A light tap on the window jarred her out of her thoughts.

Pull yourself together. She got out of the car trying to calm the shakiness in her knees. "I can't wait to get out there on the water. The river is beautiful. No matter how many times I've seen it, it never ceases to amaze me."

"Sounds nice. I think I needed this more than I realized."

She watched Trenton get a distant expression in his eyes as he looked out to the water. He looked heavy with thought, like he was finally starting to see the beauty she saw everyday. As if he realized what he was doing he turned to his car. She stepped aside while Trenton grabbed the bag she'd brought from her house. She couldn't help but stare at how his tight muscles constricted as he turned his body. *Yum!* "You don't get much time to relax in Los Angeles?" she asked.

He winked in reply turning back into his playful self. "It depends on what you consider relaxing."

Just the smallest expression from Trenton almost brought her to her knees. She wanted to melt. *It's just a wink.*

The bell over the raft rental store door rang as he held the door open for her to walk inside. As soon as the door closed he grabbed her hand, taking the lead and directing her towards the rental counter. He was such a born leader. Sidney wasn't a follower, but there was something about him that made her wonder just how far she'd be willing to go with him.

A shiver shot down her spine.

"What was that?" he asked stopping.

"What?" she asked pretending she didn't know what he was talking about while silently cursing herself for being so obvious. Really, who'd have thought he'd have felt it. She didn't think she reacted that strongly but must have for Trenton to notice.

"You know what I'm talking about, Sid. I felt your body quiver. What's going through that beautiful head of yours?"

You. How much I want you. How you set my body of fire. "Just anxious to get on the water I guess," the fib rolled off her tongue. Well it really wasn't a lie. She was excited to get out and spend the day with him. Much more excited than she should be.

"Well then I guess we better get this party started."

***

Trenton knew there was more to Sid's reaction than she wanted to tell him. He also knew when to let things go and when not too. He'd been around plenty of women to know when to push and when to let off. He'd push later, when they were alone not in the middle of a raft rental store. Then he'd be able to get the answers he wanted.

After paying for their raft, he led her out back so they could officially start their day. He couldn't wait to have her all to himself for the whole day. He wanted to get to know her better, kiss her and touch her, away from all the prying eyes of River City residents. Hopefully there wouldn't be many people out today. It sounded cheesy, but this day was about them. He wanted them both to enjoy spending time together.

"You ready for this?" he asked as he placed the raft in the water.

She threw her bag in before climbing in herself. "As ready as I'll ever be. Let's go, Stone. The water is waiting for us."

For some reason it sounded damn sexy to hear her call him by his last name. Maybe it's because none of the women he associated with at home spoke the way she did or maybe it was the clear Oregon air but something felt different here. He couldn't put his finger on what it was, but damned if he didn't plan to find out. He was an answer man and sooner or later he'd find out the mysteries of Sidney Clark.

"Yoo-hoo," She waved her hand in front of his face. "You spacing out on me or what?"

"No way, Sugar. You're too sexy to not pay attention to. I was just thinking about how much fun we're going to have out there today." He climbed in the raft behind her and pushed off. "So what's this part of the river like?"

"Most of the ride is just about relaxing and enjoying the beauties of nature. There are a few good rapids though. Nothing too dangerous but enough to get your blood flowing."

His blood was already flowing. To one specific piece of anatomy at least. "You already do that for me, Sugar. My blood flows straight to-"

"Don't even say it," Sidney cut him off. The cute little blush on her cheeks almost made him keep going. He liked to see her flushed. Too bad it was from embarrassment instead of exertion.

"Now what's the fun in that?"

"You really like embarrassing me, don't you?"

"I just like to see that pretty pink blush across your face. The cute little smile you get when I say something that turns you on even though you want to pretend it doesn't."

"Ever think you're wrong? Maybe your talk doesn't do a thing for me."

He leaned forward in the raft and captured her lips with his. Her sweet taste again engulfing him. Lightly, Trenton nibbled her bottom lip, sucking it into his mouth before he slipped his tongue inside her open mouth. Their tongues wrestled urgently, Sidney's hand pressed against his chest.

He took advantage, deepening the kiss, taking as much of her in as possible, as much as she'd let him. He felt his cock rise to attention wanting more with each sweep of his tongue. *Pull away. You can't have her like you want to in a two man raft floating down the river.* Reluctantly, Trenton pried his mouth away from hers. "I think I do as much for you as you do for me. I feel it in your kiss, the way your body awakens when I touch you. I can feel it, Sidney."

Sidney raised her eyes to look at him. She looked vulnerable. A wave of guilt swept over him.

"Yes, I want you. I think that's pretty obvious. That doesn't mean I plan to do anything about it."

She looked saddened by the admission and it tugged at his heart. He wanted her to admit her desire for him, but not at the cost of it causing her pain or strife. He only wanted to be responsible for giving her satisfaction, pleasure, joy. "Okay, we'll leave it at that for now. Tell me about your boutique," he asked changing the subject. "How'd you and Abby come about starting a New Age shop?"

She looked grateful at his words. He didn't know how or when he became able to read the expressions on her face so well, but he could. In the short couple days since he met her, he felt like he was really starting to know her. Know what she wanted, what she needed, what she liked. He could see it in her eyes, her expression, and her body language.

"Abby's mom was psychic. She never opened her own shop. It was something she did for her friends and family. She could read people like no one I've ever known. Her friends would come over and they'd have parties, that kind of thing where she'd read cards for her friends. I think it's only natural that it became Abby's passion as well."

"What about you?" He'd asked about them both, but really wanted to know more about Sidney than Abby. Nothing against her, he just wanted to know as much about the woman sitting across from him as he could.

"Well, I enjoy cards but I'm more into the Boutique part of it. The majority of the items in my shop I make myself. Not everything of course, but I make the soaps, candles, and dresses. I like to blend scents, create products to help women relax and feel beautiful. It probably sounds crazy to you, but you'd be amazed at how something as simple as a new dress, or a new scent can make a woman feel empowered and good about herself."

Yesterday he would have thought something like that sounded foolish, but the pride and joy in Sidney's voice made him believe it. She poured her heart into what she did. "It doesn't sound crazy at all. What you do is very respectable. I'd love to look at some of the things you've made some time."

The smile on her face made him forget that this was about sex. At this moment, all that mattered was making her happy.

Chapter Seven

He didn't touch her for the rest of the trip! She couldn't believe it and quite frankly it pissed her off. *This is what you want, remember? Yeah right!* It's what she knew she should want, but in reality she wanted him to strip her naked right there on the raft. Who cared about the people who sat on their docks looking out at the river? At this moment all she knew was they'd give them one hell of a show. She wanted to give them a show.

You should count your lucky stars. Instead of his ploys and plots to get her into bed they'd talked. Seriously talked. After she told him about Mystic Boutique they chatted about Abby, more about life in River City, what she like to do for fun, and even laughed about the first night they met in Portland.

He seemed genuinely interested in what she had to say. Especially about herself and River City. She wondered why he was so interested in the town, even more she wondered why he was so interested in her. The romantic in her wanted to believe it was because he liked her, really liked her not just wanted to get her into bed. Maybe he liked the town too and would visit more often.

While they rode the river, Sidney pulled out the sandwiches she'd packed for their lunch. The few minutes it took them to eat were the only moments of silence on their trip. After lunch Trenton talked about his life in Los Angeles, about his work and about the few friends he had back home.

When he spoke about his life it was like he talked about someone else. His voice was steady, detached. There was no excitement when he spoke of his friends, his world, just facts. It was so different from the Trenton she was spending the day with, the one that laughed, that asked her questions about her life.

That Trenton was more dangerous than the sex obsessed one. He was charming, sweet, and made her laugh. This Trenton she could easily fall in love with. But she'd never tell him that. And not just because she didn't want him to know how she felt. She was really starting to understand him and he wouldn't want her to point out that his softer side began to show through his harder exterior.

"We have to dock on the right up here," Sidney said pointing a finger to the end of their excursion. She didn't want the day to end and even though she knew she'd regret it later, she hoped Trenton would ask her to spend more time with him.

"Over already, huh?" he asked nonchalantly. Worry bubbled inside her. He sounded so unconcerned.

"Yep." Sitting back in the raft she tried to play it off as cool as Trenton seemed.

"It's beautiful out here. I could be here all day."

"Finally starting to see some of the beauty? Why Trenton Stone, I am surprised."

He looked her directly in the eyes. "I see a lot of beauty." Her heart pounded in her chest threatening to break free from its cage. Then he turned and broke the connection and headed toward the shore.

Trenton stepped out of the raft first before holding a hand out to her. Her limb shook as she reached up to take his strong, steadier one. When their hands clasped a zing snapped in the air around them. She couldn't explain, had never felt it before and wondered if she ever would again.

God this man is turning me into a drama queen. It was much easier to dismiss her thoughts as crazy rather than face the truth. He was special, one of a kind and he meant more to her in a short time than any man she'd ever known.

"What time is it?" he asked his deep tone penetrating her thoughts. Their hands were still united. When she glanced down she realized he'd taken off the gold watch he usually donned for their trip. Looking at her own plastic, waterproof watch, the differences in them again showed. Something as small as a watch shouldn't matter to her, but it did. He lived a different life than her. He was big city and she loved the small town. Heaviness crushed her chest.

He'll leave. He'll go home to Los Angeles and leave you broken-hearted.

Sharply, she pulled away. "Three forty-five."

His strong grasp again grabbed her hand. "I wasn't done holding that," he said then reached down to grab the raft with his free hand. "Let's get this turned in and wait for the shuttle to take us back to our car." He walked away pulling her behind him.

***

Sidney sat in near silence while they rode back to his car. Trenton let her compose herself because he knew once he told her he planned to accompany her back to her house she'd throw a fit. But the truth was he would be going no matter what. Of course he didn't plan to push himself on her, if all they did for the rest of the night was talk and spend more time together, surprisingly, it was okay with him. He needed to spend more time with her and wouldn't take no for an answer.

He enjoyed himself too much today to let it end now and no matter what she said, he knew she enjoyed herself too. When the day began all he thought about was getting her out of her cute little white shorts, but as the day went on he just liked talking and laughing with her. When he liked something he did what he had to so he could keep it. He knew he couldn't keep Sid forever, but he planned to enjoy her as long as he could.

As the van bumped along he tightened his grip on her hand. She felt good next to him, right in a way that he didn't let his overactive brain contemplate at the moment. Heat radiated off her body carrying her secret, sugary scent that he'd quickly become addicted to. Would she taste as sweet everywhere as she smelled? His body begged to know, to taste every square inch of her decadent body.

He started to get a boner right there in the van. Part of him knew he should shift and try to hide it but hiding was something he didn't do. He wanted her to know exactly what she did to him. She made him hotter than any woman ever had and hopefully tonight she'd let him experience what about her set her apart.

It isn't the sex that's going to set her apart. It's her.

Turning, Trenton looked out the window trying to give her some space. The town really was beautiful. It reminded him of home. *Home?* Where had that come from? Home was Los Angeles, not Georgia. But as he looked around he started to wonder if the life he led was really what he wanted. He felt a calmness here in River City that he hadn't felt in a long time.

He shook his head as if trying to shake the thoughts away, but they wouldn't subside. He didn't notice it until this moment. The truth struck him suddenly, but he knew they were true. He felt as drawn to this town as he did to her. *You're cracking up, Stone. You don't get drawn to places or people.* Sid would believe it. His feelings were right up her alley.

They pulled up to the rental shop where they'd left his car hours earlier. Ignoring the thoughts in his head, Trenton led her from the vehicle and to his car without a word. Getting into the Mustang she made eye contact for the first time since she'd tried to pull away when they docked. Her green eyes sparkled almost stopping his heart.

Shake it off, man. She's just a woman.

He winked at her, closed the door and walked to the driver side and climbed in.

***

"Just so you know, I'm inviting myself in," he told her when they made it to her small porch. The twinkle that sparkled in her eyes earlier was replaced by a fiery look of anger. He loved that feistiness about her. *Love? Where the hell did that word come from?*

"I'm really getting sick of this. Everything's always on your terms, Trenton. I don't understand why you're doing all this just to get into my pants."

Sure it started off that way, but that wasn't the reality of the situation anymore. Hell, he couldn't wait to get into her pants one day, but that wasn't his primary goal any longer. Couldn't she see that? Ever since he stepped into this town he'd been bending over backwards to do things her way.

"Wait a minute there, Sugar. I don't know where you've been the past few days, but it obviously isn't the planet earth." His anger shown through his words, but at the moment he didn't care.

A white haired, elderly woman next door watched them over the fence not trying to hide her nosiness. "Let's go inside," he grabbed her arm loosely.

"Now you're going to bully me?" she jerked away.

"No, I'm just trying to keep your private affairs, private," tilting his head forward he signaled that they had prying ears.

"Fine," she exhaled a deep breath before pushing the door open and letting him follow her inside.

He closed the door behind them. "Now, where were we?"

"You were insulting me by telling me I'm not living in reality or on earth as you put it." She crossed her arms across her chest and he had to fight the urge to bend down and kiss her. She was so cute when she was mad. And damn was she mad. Why couldn't she see that he just wanted to spend more time with her?

"Listen, Sid, I'm not trying to insult you, but from where I'm standing you don't know what the hell you're talking about." If he thought she had fire in her eyes before, it was nothing to the look she shot at him right now. *Wrong thing to say.* "Listen, I didn't mean that the way it sounded."

"I think you did. Maybe you better go, Trenton."

Frustrated he ran a hand through his hair, pacing her living room. "Shit. I really suck at this." It wasn't like him to admit he lacked in any area, especially when it came to women, but it was pretty damn obvious he hadn't a clue how to talk to Sidney.

"I'm not going to deny I want you," he told her. "That hasn't changed and won't. But no matter what, I won't push you. When we're together it will be because it's what we both want. Right now, I just want to spend more time with you. That's all I'm saying. Hell, we can go out again if you want. Dinner, a movie. I'm not ready to leave yet and unless you throw me out, I don't plan to."

***

She believed him. She might live to regret it, but she believed Trenton was sincere. He was a prideful man, not one to lie just to get what he wanted from someone. If he said that he just wanted to spend more time with her she could do nothing but trust him.

She felt too connected to him to believe him a liar. She'd grown to know him, to trust him, to care for him. "Why don't we stay in? I can cook dinner maybe order a movie on pay per view later if we feel like it."

Her heart pounded inside her chest while waiting for him to reply. Suddenly she wanted him to stay as much as he was determined to, but putting it into words made her vulnerable. Low self esteem wasn't her calling card, but with Trenton she couldn't understand why a man like him wanted to spend so much time with her.

What if she disappointed him? What if she wasn't what he expected? *He can't be the man for you so why does it matter?*

"We'll both cook dinner. I know my way around the kitchen," he said. She exhaled a deep breath she didn't even realize she'd been holding.

"I'd like that."

Like a kid in a candy store he grabbed her hand and headed towards her kitchen which stood right next to the living room. Though a French door separated the two, her house was small so she wasn't surprised that he would know which way to go.

They stepped into her sun-yellow kitchen. Sidney pointed to the small round table in the middle of the room signaling Trenton to sit down. "Have a seat." To her surprise he sat without another word. "I'm going to run into my room and get changed. I'll be right back."

Sidney left him in her kitchen her nerves on end. Once in her room she slipped out of her swimsuit and shorts. "What am I doing?" she asked herself. She knew this couldn't be smart, but she also knew she had to see where it would go. She couldn't live with herself if she didn't.

After slipping on a pair of black panties and bra, she sat on her bed, covering her face with her hands. *Please tell me I'm doing the right thing. Let me be able to trust the way I feel about him.* She slowly rose from the bed grabbing a pair of black sweatpants and a short, white t-shirt, putting them both on. Before she had the chance to talk herself out of whatever she was doing, Sidney headed back into the lions den.

"I have some chicken breasts in the fridge we can make. I'll pop some potatoes in the oven and make a salad. Does that sound good?" she asked after meeting him back in the kitchen.

"That sounds like the second best meal I'd like to eat today," he lifted an eyebrow when he spoke.

The heat in her body raised at least ten degrees. His innuendo sounded better to her than it should. Sidney picked up a hand towel that sat on her counter and threw it at him. "You are such a character you know that? You're lucky I'm such an easy-going woman."

Catching the towel with ease, he laughed. "Easy is the last word I would use to describe you, Sid. I think that's what makes you so special."

The appalled look on his face told her his words were as big a shock to himself as they were to her. This was the second comment he made today that insinuated she was different. She didn't know what he meant by them. No matter how easy it would be to go all girly on him she didn't plan to think they meant more than they did. Especially with the nauseous look that plastered to his face.

"Don't worry. I won't take that to mean anything more than the passing comment that I'm sure you meant it as. Like you told me in my boutique yesterday, I won't read more into any of this than what it really is." Yesterday? Was it really just yesterday that they'd started spending time together? She felt as if she'd known him forever.

~192~

"If you know anything about me Sid, I want you to know I rarely say things I don't mean. If I do, I admit to it. I can't tell you what it means, but I meant what I just said."

Her heart almost stopped. *Don't do this. Don't let yourself be fooled. Live in the moment and take this night lightly.* "Well, okay. How about we wash up and get this dinner started?"

After they cleaned their hands, Sidney grabbed the chicken out of the fridge and put it on the counter. "Can you grab the flour out of the cabinet to your right?"

Reaching up he did what she asked. When he set the bag down a cloud of flour rose from the bag and splattering on her face.

"Hey," she said wiping her face with her hand.

Trenton laughed loudly enjoying the mess he'd made.

"How do you like it?" she asked grabbing a small handful of flour from the bag and tossing it at him. She missed his face, but coated his left shoulder. His eyes spread wide with a look of shock. "What, big city boys never have food fights?" she asked grabbing another handful and tossing it at him. This time she got his neck and the side of his face.

"This means war, woman." He filled his large hand with flour and threw it at her lightly. It landed in her hair and on her face. Knowing it was coming she closed her eyes so he didn't hurt. "Ouch," lowering her face, one hand came up and covered her eye.

As planned, a quick second later Trenton was by her side. "Are you okay?" he asked cradling her face in his hands. Her body wanted to submit to him right then and there. His strength, honor, and pride could be felt in something as small as his hand on her face.

But this was a war.

Sidney slipped her free hand slowly and quietly to the bag of flour sitting on the counter. Grabbing the biggest handful she could she raised her hand to the back of his head smearing the flour in his hair. "Gotcha," she pulled away laughing.

Standing there a minute, he stared at her, a look of confusion in his eyes. "You tricked me?"

Sidney ceased her laughter long enough to reply to him. "Is this the first time someone has got the best of Trenton Stone?" Her words were meant as a joke, but he had a serious spark in his ocean colored eyes.

"As a matter of fact it is."

Guilt swept over her. The whole food fight was meant to be a game, but Trenton looked like he'd just lost a big account at work. He seemed devastated. "Trenton-" the apology almost made it from her lips when she felt a massive handful of flour smashed into the back of her head.

Her own laughter earlier was nothing compared to the booming, joyful laugh that vibrated her kitchen. She could do nothing but join him. The sound was too contagious, infectious for her not to catch the bug.

"You aren't the only one who knows how to play the game, Sid," he finally said when they stopped laughing long enough to talk. "When I play, I play to win."

Truer words had never been spoken. She knew that about him more than anything else. He'd already won her over he just didn't know it yet. The more time she spent with him the more she connected to him, she felt him deep within her soul like no other man she'd ever known. She'd feared falling in love with him and in the matter of a couple days she'd done exactly that.

She hoped she didn't come away with a broken heart.

Chapter Eight

Standing here, cooking in Sidney's bright yellow, country kitchen felt like home. He couldn't believe it. He felt more comfortable, at home than he did at his condo in LA. He was happier than he ever remembered feeling. Sidney was fun, free, and lively. She made him feel the same way and he wanted her more than ever. *It's more than that and you know it,* his inner voice told him. Ignoring it, he flipped the frying chicken while Sid continued to make the salad.

After their fight with the flour they'd each washed the majority of the white powder from their body and started the meal. They worked well together, Trenton taking care of the chicken while Sidney did the potatoes and made the salad. They chatted as they cooked, reminiscing on their day and the impromptu food fight.

She smiled a lot and he couldn't help but wonder if she was always this happy or if he somehow brought it out in her. Her body moved around the kitchen gracefully, her ass looking tight in the black sweatpants she wore. The women he knew back home wouldn't be comfortable walking around the kitchen in the comfortable attire she wore. They'd have rushed to the room dressed the part and applied a fresh face of makeup before doing a chore like cooking dinner.

Not Sid. She was a breath of fresh air and he realized he never wanted to stop breathing her in. She gave new life to his lungs, his life, and he hated to admit it, but his heart.

"The chicken about done over there?" she asked breaking into his thoughts.

"Yeah. You ready for it?" He turned his head to see her shake hers yes. He plucked the chicken from the skillet putting a piece on each plate that she'd set by him. While he moved the pan to a cooler burner, Sidney put a pile of salad and a baked potato on each plate. When she was done she walked the plates to her small table to set them down.

"I'm starving," he joined her at the table.

"Me too," she admitted as they sat down to eat.

They were each silent a few minutes, eating their food, looking up every few seconds at one another. He could sense something was on her mind. He wanted her to let it out, to feel comfortable around him to ask whatever she wanted so he continued the silence until she finally spoke.

***

"Tell me something about yourself, Trenton."

"Like what, Sid? You know who I am, where I live, what I do for a living. What else is there?"

Men. No matter how smart they were, how strong, or how confident they just didn't get it. "I want to know about *you.*" She really wanted to know more about him, everything about him, not just the basics.

"This is going to be a two way street, Sid. You get questions and so do I. Just like the first night we met, tit for tat."

Leave it to Trenton to turn this around, but at least she was getting her wish. This just might be her last opportunity to find out as much about him as she could, the big and the small. "Alright. Who goes first?"

He didn't answer, but asked his first question instead. "Tell me about Mandy the mouth. What was she talking about last night when she mentioned another out of town guy?"

Of all the questions he could ask she didn't expect that one. For all she knew, he'd completely forgotten about the incident. Why would he care about that? Unless for some reason he was the type of man who got jealous over past affairs. No, not Trenton. He was too secure to be jealous over someone in the past.

Maybe this wasn't such a good idea. His first question was a painful one, one that stood between them and what they both wanted. But man, she wanted to know more about him and this was the only way. She had to play his game to get her own rewards no matter how foolish it made her feel.

"You really want to know this? It's not that big a deal." *Yeah right.*

"Yeah right," he echoed the words she spoke in her head. How were they so in tuned to each other? She couldn't understand it.

Here goes nothing. "There was this guy who came into town on business. I know it sounds crazy that someone would come to River City on business, but it does happen. Anyway, he was here for a few months and during that time we got...close." From across the table she saw his jaw tighten and flex. *Surprise, surprise.*

"I did the typical girl thing and fell for him. I thought I meant something to him when I didn't. When it was time for him to leave he didn't even think twice about me. Not that I expected him to stay here just for me, but I thought maybe we'd try to make it work. He told me I wasn't the type of woman he could bring home to the family. Apparently the whole Mystic Boutique thing was a problem for him. Not a big enough problem so that he couldn't sleep with me though."

A deep, shaky breath escaped her lungs when she finished. She looked across the table, over their half eaten food at Trenton. He didn't look down at her or with pity. He looked like he cared and that made it a whole lot easier. It actually felt good to share it with him. Like he somehow understood her better, like their bond was strengthening.

"What a dick. You deserve better than that." The anger she heard in his voice shocked her to the core. "If he ever comes back into town I want you to show me who he is. I'll show him what's good for him."

Her heart soared with the protective tone in his voice. *Get your butt back down to earth, girl. He'll be leaving soon too.* Changing the subject she asked her question. "What's the real reason you ran away from your hometown when you were eighteen?"

Trenton cut a piece of chicken and popped it into his mouth. He chewed for a minute, swallowed and then looked her in the eye. He looked apprehensive but spoke anyway. "You sure you want to hear this?"

"Yes," her voice sounded shaky. Like she was the one telling some big secret from her past.

"I grew up with money. We were high respected citizens in town. Unfortunately, no one knew our little secret. My dad was a drug addict. He not only did drugs, but he sold them as well. He hid it well. Hell, my mom hid it for him. It used to piss me off that she let him get away with it. She wanted everyone to look up to us and she never once pushed him to get help because he was her paycheck.

"I hated them both for it. Hated that they cared so much what other people thought they'd live a lie. I know it was an addiction. I don't look down at people for that, but I can't handle the fact that he never tried to get help. She never cared about him or me enough to make him. All she cared about was what everyone else thought."

Trenton stopped and took a couple deep breaths before continuing. "A couple weeks before I turned eighteen my dad won a citizenship award in town. I remember watching him except the award, looking at all the people who held adoration in their eyes and I was sick. I couldn't handle it anymore. To make a long story short, I turned eighteen and left to find something better. I swore I'd never care what other people thought about me. I'd never make that the most important thing in my life."

Wow. She didn't know what she expected, but that wasn't it. Her heart went out to him she respected him and understood him much better now. "I'm so sorry, Trenton."

He looked at her. His eyes were soft, caring. "Don't be. I didn't tell you so you would feel bad for me. It wasn't so bad and I've had a great life in LA. I told you because I trust you."

If she doubted it before right now she knew without a shadow of a doubt that she loved him. Loved everything about him. The fact that he honored her with his trust, with memories that had to be painful for him almost brought her to tears. But he wouldn't want that so she would hold back. "What's your next question?"

"It's a tough one. You sure you're ready for it?"

Not really. "Throw it at me. I didn't expect you to go easy on me, Stone."

"Why do you really keep turning me down?"

Sidney stalled returning his earlier tactic by taking a bite of her food. His question didn't surprise her. Trenton was blunt. She expected nothing less than that and she actually respected that quality about him. Honesty was important to her so she'd be truthful with him but she wondered if he was ready to hear what she had to say.

"You sure you want to know, Stone?"

"I think I can handle anything you throw at me, Sid."

"Well I'm sure you know part of it comes from Ivan, the guy I told you about. But the real truth of the matter is I know you can hurt me ten times as much as he ever did. I can't explain it, but from the second I saw you I knew you were different. I knew you could break my heart."

The words passed through her lips with authority. She was tired of running. Trenton meant something to her. Exactly what, she didn't know, but it was big. Luckily, he didn't flinch at her words. He just nodded his head and waited for her next question.

Here goes nothing. "Did you find what you were looking for when you left?"

The silence that coated the air sat thicker than the silences before. She wondered if she made a mistake by asking the question, but no matter what, she wouldn't take it back. This was the only way to find out all she could about Trenton. Somehow she already felt as though she knew him better than anyone else, but she wanted to know him completely.

"No," his blunt honesty didn't surprise her. "I was happy, sure, but I don't think I realized I hadn't found what I was looking for until now."

***

He didn't plan to say the words but they'd drifted from his mouth nonetheless. They were true, he knew it as he said them, but he hadn't planned it. No matter what the truth was he still didn't know what he planned to do about it. Talking with Sidney felt different than anything he'd ever known. She was smart, strong, funny, special...his. His primitive, possessive nature emerged from him with a force.

But still, could he stay in River City to be with her? He wasn't sure and no matter what, he didn't know if he was capable of putting someone else before himself. *Selfish bastard.*

Sidney pushed her plate to the middle of the table and stood up. She walked toward him with an air of confidence that reminded him of himself.

"Come here, Trenton." For the first time in his life he found himself submitting to what someone else ordered without a fight. He wanted to go to her.

They met in the middle. Sidney reached around his neck and stood on her toes to kiss him. He'd never felt a sweeter pleasure. Taking over, his tongue dove into her mouth showing her exactly how powerfully she affected him. He was ravenous, but not for food. He wanted something only Sidney could give to him.

Lifting her up, Sidney wrapped her legs around his waist their kiss never breaking. He possessed her mouth as he dreamed about possessing her body. She responded beautifully, like a blissfully turned on woman. *Do you want to hurt her? You're planning on leaving her behind.*

Pulling his lips away sharply Trenton walked her over to the counter and set her down, his forehead leaning against the cabinet behind her. His body shook with uncontrollable lust.

"What's wrong?" her sweet little voice asked.

He couldn't believe he was going to do this. He'd never wanted a woman like he wanted Sid, but suddenly he grew a conscience and couldn't imagine hurting her. He couldn't make love to her knowing it would break her heart when he went back to LA. "I want you so fucking badly, Sid." His words sounded weak. A sound he'd never heard from his own mouth.

"I'm offering myself to you. I'm not strong enough to deny you anymore."

Exactly what he didn't want to hear. "I can't believe I'm saying this, but we can't do it. It's not right."

He stepped away so he could look her in the eyes. Big mistake. Pain shown in her eyes assaulting his heart. Before he knew it his cheek stung, her hand slapping him.

"Goddamn you, Trenton! It always has to be your way, everything on your terms, doesn't it? You want me, I tell you no and you push and push. When I decide I can't hold back anymore and try to give you what you want, you don't want it anymore." He let her push him away and watched her leap down from the counter.

Her pain reached to his soul, almost unbearable. It was like they were somehow connected. "Wait," he grabbed her arm when she tried to walk away. "Don't walk away from me right now. You have no idea what you're saying."

"No, Trenton. I'm tired of doing everything you say. I'm done. I think you better leave."

He didn't let her go. "Tired of doing everything I want? You're the first person since I was eighteen years old who doesn't do what I want. Yet, here I am."

Their eyes met and held. "Why are you here? If you don't want me anymore you could save us both a lot of hassle by just going."

How could she think he didn't want her? "I could explode from my need to be inside you right now, Sid. I'm on fire for you. My body aches to know how it would feel to slip inside your warmth."

A single tear slowly trickled down her cheek. "Then why won't you take me?"

Trenton groaned running his free hand through his hair. "Because I can't promise you anymore than that. When I leave I don't want to hurt you." He couldn't bear to hurt her.

First she looked pained like his words cut her, but then she smiled a weak, yet confident smile. "When you leave I'll be hurt whether we're together or not, Trenton. But I can't imagine letting you go without knowing what its like to make love to you. I need you."

Chapter Nine

A man could only be so strong and he'd met his limit. Hell, he'd left it in the dust. The need to have her was too overwhelming. Hearing her utter the words, "I need you" pushed him over the edge. Without another thought he brought his lips down to meet hers. Eagerly she met his kiss with authority.

They kissed like they were the only two people in the world, like their lives depended on it. Her tongue tangled with his, urging her way into his mouth. On reflex he sucked it deeper into his mouth enjoying the way she molded her body against his and moaned into his mouth. Wrapping his arms around her, Trenton dug his hand into her bouncy blond curls.

"You have flour in your hair," he whispered against her mouth. "I feel bad. Let me wash you." He didn't form his words as a question. He planned to do everything with her tonight, to explore each other's bodies completely. Sidney replied with another moan. Taking control, he lifted her in his arms, kissing her again as he carried her down the hall.

"Which door?" he murmured.

"Right."

He took her words to mean the first door on the right and turned in to find a small, tidy, bathroom. With an urgency he'd never felt Trenton stepped into the shower with Sidney in his arms, clothes and all.

"Ah," Sidney screamed as he turned the cold water on them. "It's too cold."

"Is it? I'm so hot for you right now I didn't notice." He held her body up between his own and the shower wall before reaching to add some hot water. "Is this better?"

She replied by kissing him again. The water soaked them making her clothes form tightly against her body. Unable to hold himself back, Trenton let her slide down the wall so she could hold herself up and explored her body with his hands. He wanted to know every inch of her. She felt warm and supple. Soft and feminine.

With shaky hands he moved to the tie in her sweats. They loosened easily. "I need to see you naked, Sid." Turning her so that she stood under the spray, he dropped to his knees in front of her. Hooking his fingers in the sides of her sweats and panties, Trenton began to pull them down her smooth, white legs. He went slowly, trying to savor this moment. The task wasn't easy, but he was a determined man.

Trenton worked them down her legs, throwing them out of the shower. Her blond curls gleaned for him. "Just as sexy as I imagined," he said running his hands up and down her legs. The same freckles that graced her nose spotted her legs here and there. Not a large amount, just a few cute little brown spots. He wanted to kiss them all.

After he finished getting her naked.

Reaching up he unbuttoned her plain white shirt, pulling it down her arms. She looked so beautiful looking down at him, anticipation in her eyes, water streaming down her body. *I love you.* The words echoed in his head. At this moment he wasn't surprised by them. He'd denied it to himself since the first time he laid eyes on her.

Sidney unhooked the front clasp on her bra. Her large breasts popped out, pink nipples beckoned him, sparkling with water. Unable to stop himself he rose to his feet, sucking one pert nipple into his mouth. Heaven. She tasted like the sweetest candy, like passion, pleasure, happiness all wrapped into one decedent treat.

"Oh God," she said enthusiastically. Her words urged him on. Trenton sucked her nipple with care, nipping it lightly, drawing it deeply into his mouth while he teased the other breast with his hand.

"How did I ever wait this long to taste you?" he asked before moving his mouth to her other breast to enjoy it as well.

"My fault. Won't happen again." Her words were spoken breathlessly. It was the sexiest sound he'd ever heard.

Trenton left her breast and began kissing his way down her body. He lingered on her soft stomach, slipping his tongue inside her belly button. His lips caressed her hips, kissing a lone freckle he saw on her right hip bone.

"Beautiful." In a mere second he had his mouth on her, tasting her sweetest spot. Sidney moved to lean against the wall, Trenton on his knees following her. The water beat down on them, but he hardly noticed. All that mattered was Sid and giving her pleasure.

She panted above him. "Trenton," his name whispered from her mouth and went straight to his heart. "I can't take it. Too much."

He looked up at her. Passion ignited in her eyes fueling him. "You can take it, Sid. I promised you pleasure and I'll be damned if we stop now."

"No, can't stop." He hardly heard her words as he again began to kiss her. With one hand he spread her lips apart and slowly licked from bottom to top. "Delicious." Just like he knew she would be. He felt her body shake, quiver as she stood there letting him feast from her. Her hands worked their way into his hair urging him to keep going.

His tongue lapped at her, taking in her essence as he dove his tongue in and out. He felt her grip in his hair tighten as she pushed him closer. Damn, he knew she'd be hot. She was a wildcat waiting to be set free. Thank God she let him.

"Trenton," she screamed his name and pulled his hairs that she firmly gripped, then came in a shattering climax.

Getting to his feet he held her while her body shook lightly in aftershocks. "This is just the beginning, Sid. I have so much more in store for you." He brought his lips down to kiss the crease between her neck and shoulder. "But I promised to wash you first so I will."

He wanted to free himself so badly. His body hard and ready to explode beneath his constricting, wet clothes. If he did, he'd never get through these next few minutes of pampering her.

"I want you." His cock jutted in his pants when she spoke.

"You'll have me, Sugar. Just wait a few more minutes." Trenton moved her away from the spray of water and turned her so she faced away from him. Grabbing the bottle of strawberry vanilla shampoo he squeezed a small amount in his hands and gently began rubbing it into her hair.

"That feels good. I've never had a man wash my hair before."

"Good. No one else is worthy to have their hands on you, Sidney. Only me." He knew the words sounded foolish. She wasn't his, but damned if he could hold them in. He didn't want to hold them in. He wanted her to be his. She would be his by the time they were done.

She didn't reply to his statement so he continued rubbing the shampoo into her hair. When he felt sure all the flour was out he moved her back under the spray. "Close your eyes," he commanded. She did as he told her looking sexy and submissive as he rinsed her hair clean.

Turning off the water, he helped her from the shower grabbing a fluffy towel off her rack and wrapping it around her. He then made quick work of his wet clothes removing them. Before tossing his pants to the floor he grabbed a couple silver packets from his pocket.

"Wow," he hadn't even realized Sidney was staring until she spoke. Her mouth gapped open as she stared at his hard cock.

"You like what you see?" he asked knowing the answer. She licked her lips in reply. "I can't wait anymore." He lifted Sidney into his arms and carried her through the only other door in her hallway. Across the room was a large, waiting bed. He couldn't wait to use it.

***

Her body pulsed, throbbed, begged for more of Trenton's attention. When he said he promised her pleasure she had no idea just how much he had in store for her. Their shower was the most erotic moment of her life and from what he said it was just the beginning. She couldn't wait to see what else he had in store for her.

Trenton laid her down on her deep purple plush comforter. It had always reminded her of something royalty would have. She felt like royalty when her emperor laid her down.

"Open your legs." He sounded just as demanding as ever only this time she couldn't wait to do what he told her. Leaning back against the pillows she spread her legs for him. Desire set in his eyes. Her body pulsed more knowing that she put the look there.

After he looked his fill, he finally brought his long, strong body down lying between her legs before he brought his lips to hers once again. He was strength personified. Hot and gorgeous and for the next, who knew how long, he was hers. He kissed her sensuously, slowly and with care. Her breast tingled, her heart soared.

Her body begged to learn every hard plane of his, each rigid line, each sculpted muscle. Her hands started their journey on his shoulders and worked their way down. He radiated so much heat she felt singed. She loved this man, knew it with every fiber of her being. Probably had always known it, but feared what admitting it would do to her heart.

How she'd fallen so quick, she didn't know, but as he kissed her, his lips trailing down her neck, nipping her sensitive skin, her heart knew he was the one and only for her. When he sucked her nipple into his mouth she nearly came for the second time in one night.

"I can't keep my mouth off you, Sid. You taste so sweet, so addictive."

"I don't want you to keep your mouth off me. You feel so good, Trenton." He continued to suckle her tender breasts switching back and forth.

"I've been a patient man," he said his mouth making her breasts feel lonely. "But I can't wait anymore."

"Don't," she told him while he ripped open one of the packets he brought with him. She'd never been so blunt with a man, but couldn't imagine it any other way with Trenton. She felt too comfortable with him to mix words.

Sitting up Sidney got another look at his long, velvety length as he covered himself with the condom. Every inch of him shouted strength and power.

"I can't wait to feel myself inside you." He came down and slowly pushed the head of his cock inside her waiting body. "Look at me."

She couldn't help but obey. When their eyes where locked he pushed himself deeply inside her. Sidney gasped as he buried himself to the hilt.

"Oh God." They were the only words she could bring herself to say. So many others floated through her head, but nothing else found its way from her lips. She wanted to tell him she loved him, but at this moment all she could think about was how perfect he felt inside her.

It was a tight, but perfect fit and when he started to pump inside her she knew what it felt like to be in heaven, in her very own utopia that she never wanted to leave.

"You're mine Sidney," he said as he pumped in and pulled out of her. She couldn't think straight enough to dissect his words. Not right now. Her nails dug into his back, but she knew it wouldn't hurt him, not Trenton so she let herself do as her body told her

"Say it Sidney. Say you're mine," he ordered.

"I'm yours." The words were automatic. Even though he only meant sexually, to her, she would always be his.

He moved faster, her body bursting in ways she'd never experienced before. He slid in and out her heartbeat matching his thrusts. They were so in tuned. Just when she knew she couldn't hold her climax back any longer, Trenton leaned down to whisper in her ear as he buried himself inside her again.

"Come, Sidney." The second the words left his mouth the flood gates opened. Her body climaxed with a power that she didn't know she had inside her. Trenton followed right behind.

***

He wrapped his arms around her holding her tightly. She felt more at home in her own house than she ever had which made no sense. This had been her home for years except now it felt different, better with Trenton here holding her. *Don't let yourself do this. You're going to cause yourself more pain in the end.*

Yet she couldn't help it. Though she knew this wasn't the kind of place for Trenton, she wasn't the type of woman to hold him, yet she wished it all the same. Maybe it was his sex talk that had her mind dreaming about things she knew would never be. But then she knew that wasn't the case. She'd want him to stay no matter if he'd made her feel like he cared for her or not.

Rolling over she looked him in the eyes. He looked distant, a far off expression on his face. He regretted it. She could see it in his eyes.

"I'm staying." His voice was deep, scratchy. Her body jolted upwards in surprise when he spoke.

"Don't, Trenton. Don't make me promises you can't keep. I know you don't really want to be here."

"Don't tell me what I want, Sid. I'm staying. I'm not hurting you like that asshole did."

So there it was. He felt guilty because he'd made love to her and would be leaving. She couldn't let him stay, not for that reason even though she wanted nothing more than to see his blue eyes everyday.

"I'm not that weak. You don't have to stay just because you're afraid of hurting me. I knew what I was getting myself into." Feeling self conscience she covered her bare breast with her hands.

"Don't cover yourself from me. Not after all we've been through the past few days."

Had it only been a few days? It felt like an eternity. She didn't know what to feel, what to say. She wanted him to stay, but not just because he felt bad and didn't want to hurt her. "You can't stay."

"You can't stop me."

Sidney left the bed taking the blanket with her to cover herself. "Stop being so...you. I know this isn't what you want, yet you're pushing to do it just to have control."

"If you think that, you don't know me at all, Sid." He stood stalking around, anger in his step, not paying any attention to his own nudeness.

"I know you. That's why I can't let you stay."

"And I know you. That's why I can't leave. I know you better than I've ever known anyone and I can't imagine my life without you. I love you, Sidney."

***

She looked like she might faint. Briefly he wondered if he should have eased into his admission. The words sounded so much more real when he said them aloud so he couldn't imagine how she must be feeling. Part of him couldn't believe he said them, but he was glad he did. It was the first time he'd ever said the words to another woman and he was glad it was her. Sid was different. She deserved his love, she deserved more.

"Don't," she stuttered. "Don't say that unless you mean it." Her hand came up and covered her mouth.

"I'm not saying out of obligation because we slept together. I love you." He couldn't help but say it again.

"How can you? I'm not the kind of woman for a guy like you. This isn't the place for a guy like you."

He looked hurt. "Don't tell me what I feel and what's best for me. I've felt more at home these past two days than I have for a long time, maybe ever."

A faint smile started to form on her beautiful face. "Really?"

"Yes, Sidney. You know me better than that. I always say what I mean and I'm staying."

"Whether I like it or not?" She said her smile growing.

"Yes. I can't leave you. Not now."

"Well then I guess we better be glad I want you to stay more than I've ever wanted anything in my whole life. I love you too, Trenton."

She rushed at him, slamming herself against him and hugged him tightly. He felt more complete than he ever had.

Then he kissed her. Taking in her sweetness like he would for the rest of his life. "Say it, Sidney," he said the same words he'd used early. He needed to hear it again. "Say you're mine."

"I'm yours, Trenton. Forever, I'm yours."

***

They made love twice more before Trenton fell asleep holding her. Her body felt weak, drained, but she couldn't sleep. Her mind ran too wild, her heart too excited to slow down. Slipping from under his heavy arm, Sidney put on a long t-shirt and walked into her living room.

Without a thought to the time she picked the phone up and dialed Abby.

"Hey Sid." Abby said before she could speak.

She knew her friend didn't have caller ID. "Expecting my call?"

"I'm your best friend. Who else would you call to share the good news with?"

Sidney didn't ask how her friend knew her news before she told her. "Did you know from the beginning?"

"I knew something special would happen for you, but I didn't know the extent of it until he came to the boutique. It only took one look in his eyes to know."

Her heart raced. "I'm so happy Abbs. I hope-"

Abby cut her off. "Don't say it. Everything will work out, Sidney. He's your destiny, your soul mate.

About the Author

Kelley Nyrae has loved writing for as long as she can remember. From the moment she won her first writing contest in the third grade she knew writing was her passion. Her plan had always been to write children's books but for one reason or another it never worked out. In 2005 she became a stay at home mom for the first time. That's when she picked up her first romance novel and fell in love. She knew that writing romance books is what she was meant to do and her life hasn't been the same ever since.

Kelley has been blessed with a wonderful, supportive husband and two beautiful children who always bring a smile to her face. She resides in sunny Southern California.

Printed in the United States
112431LV00001B/28-30/P